*"I don't make off*

Something about the hu warmth in Quint's eyes, sent prickles of excitement racing through Maura. She could feel her cheeks growing warm and pink and she suddenly felt like a foolish teenager instead of a woman who'd been married and divorced.

But just for this once, she wasn't going to think about the dangers this man represented to her peace of mind. Tomorrow she would remind herself that she was behaving like an idiot. Today she was going to let herself enjoy the pleasure of being in the presence of a very sexy man.

Dear Reader,

Most often the characters I write about are clear in my mind. I know every detail about them and what makes them tick. But Quint Cantrell was an enigma to me. He loves his family, yet keeps to himself. He has lots of money, though he doesn't particularly like having it. He could live in a mansion. Instead he makes his home in a run-down ranch house. And though he's considered one of the most eligible bachelors around, he prefers the company of his horse.

The man appeared happy, so why bother stirring him up? Because I, like his grandfather Abe, finally realized that Quint was missing the most important thing in life— love. 'Course, a man like Quint is bound to rebel. After all, he knows what he wants—or does he?

I hope you'll travel with me again to the rugged southwest to see the twists and turns that Quint takes before he finally learns to share his heart.

God bless the trails you ride,

*Stella*

# BRANDED WITH HIS BABY

## STELLA BAGWELL

Silhouette®

## SPECIAL EDITION®

Published by Silhouette Books

America's Publisher of Contemporary Romance

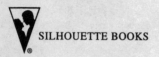

**SILHOUETTE BOOKS**

ISBN-13: 978-0-373-65500-7

BRANDED WITH HIS BABY

Recycling programs
for this product may
not exist in your area.

Copyright © 2010 by Stella Bagwell

Visit Silhouette Books at www.eHarlequin.com

**Printed in U.S.A.**

**Titles by Stella Bagwell**

## STELLA BAGWELL

has written more than seventy novels for Silhouette Books. She credits her loyal readers and hopes her stories have brightened their lives in some small way.

A cowgirl through and through, she loves to watch old Westerns, and has recently learned how to rope a steer. Her days begin and end helping her husband care for a beloved herd of horses on their little ranch located on the south Texas coast. When she's not ropin' and ridin', you'll find her at her desk, creating her next tale of love.

The couple have a son, who is a high school math teacher and athletic coach.

To my sissy, Thelma Foster.
To have a sister like you is to be truly blessed.
I love you.

## Chapter One

The moment Quint Cantrell walked through the door of his grandfather's ranch house, he got the eerie feeling that something was wrong.

At this time of the early evening Abe was usually watching the news on the small television situated in a corner of the cozy living room. Instead, the old man's leather recliner was empty and the TV screen was black.

Uneasy, Quint started to call out, but stopped as he caught the sound of a radio coming from the direction of the kitchen. As he quickly strode toward the back of the house, he realized with another start that the singer was Billie Holiday.

What the heck was going on around this place? His grandfather liked music, but certainly not that kind! And the house held the peculiar scent of roses instead of pipe tobacco and old boots.

Rounding the open doorway to the kitchen, he practically skidded to a halt as he spotted a woman standing at the cabinet counter. Yesterday, while he'd been eating lunch at the Blue Mesa, a family acquaintance had stopped by his table and mentioned that a rumor was going around about a woman staying out at Apache Wells. Quint had laughingly dismissed the idea as nothing more than a wild rumor. Since his grandmother had passed away fifteen years ago, the only females who ever stepped foot in this house were Quint's mother or sister. Hell freezing over would be more likely to happen than a woman living in Abe's house. Or so Quint had believed.

Stunned by this turn of events, Quint stared.

Tall and slender with hair the color of a black cherry hanging nearly to her waist, she was dressed casually in blue jeans and a green Western shirt with darker green flowers dotting the yokes and cuffs. If her face looked anything like her backside, Quint decided, she was definitely a pretty woman.

"Uh—excuse me, ma'am."

Obviously surprised by the sound of his voice, the woman whirled around to stare at him. Her dark eyes were wide, and her lips parted as she took a halting step in his direction.

"Oh! I didn't realize anyone had come in," she said in a breathy voice. "You gave me a fright."

He stepped forward and even though his gaze was focused solely on her, he knew his grandfather wasn't in the room. He also realized his initial guess had been correct. The woman was pretty—though quietly so. Like a violet hidden beneath a clump of sagebrush, it might take a second look to find the beauty, but it was there.

"I could say the same about you," he replied, his eyes sliding over her face. She appeared vaguely familiar. "It's not every day I walk into my grandfather's house and find a woman. Who are you, anyway?"

Her lips, which were full and dusky pink, twisted ever so slightly. "I'm sorry. I urged Abe to warn you about me, but you know that he pretty much does things his own way. He wanted me to be a surprise," she said with a mixture of amusement and regret. "As to who I am, I thought you might recognize me. But I suppose I've been away from Lincoln County too long for you to remember."

So his earlier assumption had been right. He had met the woman before. But where? he wondered, as his gaze scanned her dark green eyes, high cheekbones and heart-shaped face. She was definitely easy to look at, he realized, and then his memory kicked in like a startled mule. Hellfire, she was one of the Donovan bunch! A rich, rough and rowdy family that owned a notable horse farm down in the Hondo Valley.

"I remember now," he said. "You're one of the Donovan brood. A nurse. You were at the hospital when my sister had her baby."

She inclined her head forward. "That's right. I'm Maura—second oldest of six siblings. You've probably seen us around from time to time."

Shrugging, he wondered why her suggestion made him feel like a recluse. "I don't do much socializing anymore. But I know your brothers and sisters. Bridget is my mother's doctor."

She nodded. "Bridget is very good at her job. And very busy."

Folding his arms against his chest, Quint glanced beyond her shoulder to where a pot of something was simmering on the stove. It was filling the whole room with the scent of chicken and spices. Where was Jim, the old bunkhouse cook who usually prepared his grandfather's meals? And why in the world would a Donovan be here at his grandfather's ranch?

"Yesterday, when someone in town told me that a woman was staying on the ranch, I practically called him a liar." Quint shook his head as he tried to assemble the questions running rampant in it. "I don't mean to sound meddlesome, but why are you here? And where is Gramps?"

Her breasts rose and fell as she drew in a deep breath, then blew it out. His questions appeared to make her uncomfortable, which only roused his curiosity even more.

"Abe is down at the ranch yard visiting with the hands," she answered. "And I'm here because I live here now. With your grandfather, as his nurse."

If she'd whacked Quint's shins with an ax handle, the shock couldn't have been any greater. He sputtered. "His nurse!"

"That's right," she said smoothly, then quickly added, "Excuse me, would you? I need to tend to the soup."

Dazed by her revelation, Quint watched her turn to the cookstove, where she stirred a bubbling pot with a wooden spoon. Her movements seemed so casual, that he got the feeling she'd been here long enough to feel at home.

Two weeks had passed since he'd taken the time to drive to Apache Wells, but he'd talked on the phone to his grandfather several times and nothing had been mentioned about a nurse, or any need for one. She'd said that Abe had wanted to surprise him. Well, the old man had done that and more, Quint thought.

Walking farther into the room, Quint lifted the gray Stetson from his head and raked a hand through his curly hair. He'd had a day that would try a saint, and he wasn't in the mood for beating around the bush.

"Okay, is this one of my grandfather's outlandish jokes? Abe doesn't need a nurse. He's as healthy as a horse."

"Is that what you think?" she asked politely.

"Hell, yes!" he blurted out, then stabbed his fingers through his hair again and added in a calmer tone, "I mean of course, I do. Gramps went for a checkup about three weeks ago. The man pronounced Abe as fit as a fiddle. Or is there something I need to know?"

"I doubt that. Abe says you're aware of his vertigo problem."

Putting down the spoon, she turned to face him and Quint was knocked for a loop all over again. Of the three Donovan sisters, he was least familiar with this one. If his calculations were right, she'd finished high school a few years ahead of him. Which would make her midthirties— though she sure didn't look five or six years older than his twenty-nine. He recalled hearing, a long time ago, that she'd moved away and married some man from Albuquerque. But from the look of her empty ring finger— Quint told himself he didn't know why he had looked there first—her marital status had changed along with her residence.

"I'm aware that he has dizzy spells," Quint replied. "But the way I understand it, the condition isn't life-threatening and it only hits him occasionally."

"If a spell of vertigo caused him to suffer a bad fall, it could be life-threatening."

"Sorry, Ms. Donovan, but I could suffer a fall walking across the backyard. Any of us could."

"The likelihood of that happening skyrockets when a person's head is spinning."

Quint couldn't argue that point. He'd been with his grandfather when one of these spells hit him and the old man had been unable to walk without someone to assist him.

"So? I'd rather see him die than to chain him to a chair. And you can't go around holding onto his arm all day. In fact, I doubt you could keep up with him," Quint added.

She sighed. "Abe isn't a young man anymore, you know."

Quint bristled. He didn't want anyone insinuating that Abe was getting old and decrepit. He wasn't. And Quint refused to let anyone make him believe otherwise.

"Eighty-four may sound old to you," Quint said to her, "but trust me, Gramps has the mind and the body of a man twenty years younger."

"I agree with that."

His expression turned incredulous. "If you know that, then what the hell are you doing here?"

She walked forward and leaned a hip against the edge of a chrome-and-Formica dining table. Quint couldn't help but notice the sensual curve of her breasts and waist, the way her dark red hair waved against her pale cheek. He didn't recall Maura Donovan as being so sexy. But back before she'd left the area, he'd only had eyes for Holly. Lovely, fickle Holly.

"Are you angry because I'm living here?" she asked.

Was he? The question jarred him almost as much as the sight of her. No. He wasn't angry. He was confused, shaken and a bit hurt that Abe hadn't seen fit to consult him about hiring Maura Donovan. But then, his grandfather had always been a maverick. The only person he'd ever answered to was his late wife, Jenna. There was no reason for Quint to think Abe needed or wanted his grandson's opinion.

"I'm not angry. I'm confused. Abe isn't sick. And there's no way you can protect him from a dizzy spell. So why did he hire you?"

A faint smile tilted the corners of her lips and it suddenly dawned on Quint that it was the first semblance of warmth he'd seen on her face since he'd walked into the room. The subtle expression softened her features and he found himself looking at things about her that had nothing to do with anything. Like her skin that was all smooth and pink and pearly.

Hell, what had she done to Abe? he wondered. Batted her long lashes at him and smiled? He could see how a young man would succumb to this woman's charms. Quint was feeling the effects of her presence himself. But Abe? Sure, his grandfather was still a man, but he'd always been so crazy in love with his late wife that he'd never looked twice at another woman. But maybe she did something to change that, Quint thought.

"Your grandfather suffers from benign paroxysmal positional vertigo. When it happens I can help him with the exercises and head maneuvers he needs to do in order to get over it. And see that he takes his medication, whenever it's needed. Having a nurse close by makes him feel safe and cared for. Surely you wouldn't want to deny the man that much?"

Shaking his head with resignation, Quint pulled out one of the dining chairs and flopped down on the seat. He'd been building fences all day. Sweat and dirt stained his shirt and jeans and he was tired enough to sleep for a week. He wasn't in any shape to argue with Maura Donovan. And maybe he shouldn't be arguing, he thought wearily. Maybe he should just thank his lucky stars that Abe was being looked after on a daily basis.

"I didn't realize nurses also cooked for their patients," he said, his gaze straying to the simmering pot on the stove, then back to her.

He watched faint color warm her cheeks and then his gaze dropped to her lips. She didn't appear to wear lipstick. But then, she didn't need to. Her lips were already dark and moist and the idea of biting into them, kissing them, flashed through his mind, shocking him with the totally erotic thought.

"I understand that before I came Jim did all the cooking around here, but I offered to take over because—" Pausing, she wrinkled her nose. "Well, neither man was eating a healthy diet. Red meat and potatoes was about all I could find around here."

"That's what Gramps likes," Quint said automatically while he pushed his mind to more pertinent issues. How long was she planning on staying here and was she thinking to get more out of his grandfather than just nurse's wages? The Donovans were wealthy people. If Maura never worked a day in her life, she could still live in luxury. So why would she want to hide herself away here on Apache Wells? Abe's ranch was remote, with the nearest neighbor—an old woman everyone called Crazy Gertie—fifteen miles away. Gertie was someone who'd been known to take potshots at anyone who decided to come near the shack she lived in. As for his grandfather, Abe could be charming whenever he chose to be, but for the most part he was set in his ways and didn't hesitate to speak his mind. A young, beautiful woman like Maura wouldn't deliberately choose to spend her days like this unless there was something in it for her, would she?

The questions were really none of Quint's business and probably totally out of line. But damn it, Abe was his grandfather! Someone had to look out for the old man's security. Two years ago his sister had married a Texas Ranger and moved to his ranch near San Antonio. A month ago, Alexa had given birth to daughter Jessica. Add her to the couple's toddler son, J.D., and his sister's life was consumed with caring for her own family. That left only Quint and his mother, Frankie, to keep an eye on their aging relative.

"What we like and what's good for us aren't always the same, Mr. Cantrell."

Amen to that, he thought drily. "My grandfather never was one to follow rules—good or bad."

And Maura figured the man sitting at the small dining table wasn't much of a rule follower, either. He'd said he wasn't angry about her being here, yet she could see doubts and questions unfolding like a picture show across his rough-hewn face.

Well, she couldn't blame the man. She'd had her own doubts about taking this job. But Abe had been persistent. He'd also come along with the proposition at just the right time. She'd loved her job at Sierra General Hospital. Helping ailing patients get back on their feet was something she'd always wanted and needed to do since she'd become a nurse nearly fourteen years ago. But recently Dr. Weston's uninvited pursuit of her had turned the job she'd once cherished into a walking nightmare. On the whole he was a nice man and an excellent doctor, but he'd refused to believe she didn't want to see him romantically. His attention hadn't quite crossed over to harassment, but it was making her a bit uncomfortable. So she'd spent the past two months running around the hospital trying to dodge the man.

Turning back to the cabinet counter, she began to gather makings for a fresh pot of coffee while she attempted to convince herself that Quint Cantrell wasn't making her heart beat fast, her mouth go dry. She'd not expected him to look so raw and sexy, so much a man. Even with her back to him, she could easily visualize the rusty-brown color of his hair, the sky-blue of his eyes and the strong, stubborn square of his jaw.

Taking a deep breath, she said, "When Abe approached me a few weeks ago, he was going through tests to find the cause of his vertigo. He told me then that he was afraid of falling and breaking a bone."

Quint snorted. "What a bunch of bull. Gramps has never been afraid of falling. Why, only a few weeks ago, he rode a green broke horse on roundup. The thing reared up and fell over backward with him. Do you think that scared him? Hell, no. He climbed back on and rode the animal that day and the rest of the week."

Pausing in the middle of her task, Maura glanced over her shoulder at him and as her eyes settled on his face, some subtle thing fluttered in the pit of her stomach. She'd never been properly introduced to Quint Cantrell, but their families had often traveled in the same circles and she recalled seeing him a few times oh so many years ago. He'd been a handsome young guy then, one that as a teenager, her younger sister Bridget had swooned over. But according to Bridget, he'd never given her the time of day. Instead he'd steadily dated Holly Johnson and everyone in Lincoln and Ortero Counties had believed the two would eventually get married. Maura had never heard what happened with the couple, but she'd heard nasty rumors. But then, Maura knew all too well that most breakups were ugly.

"I'm hardly saying your grandfather is scared," she said quietly. "I think—well, I think you should ask him yourself why he believes he needs a nurse. As for me, I'm very happy to be here. Abe is—" She broke off with a fond smile. "He's quite a character, and I'll be honest, I've already fallen a little in love with him."

His lips pressed into a thin line of disapproval, but Maura told herself she didn't care what this man was thinking. Let him think what he wanted. Her relationship with Abe was between the old man and her.

"I didn't think nurses were supposed to become emotionally involved with their patients," he said.

Turning back to the cabinet counter, she poured water into the coffeemaker, then shoved the carafe in place. "That's right. But I have a heart in my chest, not a rock. And it has a mind of its own."

He didn't make any sort of reply and after a few moments, the air in the kitchen felt so tense that she had to turn and face him. Yet the sardonic expression she expected to see wasn't there. Instead, she was jolted by his sober blue gaze honing in on her like a microscope.

"Abe tells me that you've been developing more of your family land," she said as casually as she could.

"Gramps purchased the property over near Capitan more than twenty years ago and since then has done little with it. For some reason, he thinks I can make something out of the place."

He didn't go on to tell her that the property was the only Cantrell land that belonged solely to Quint. Along with that, it possessed some of the finest grazing land in southern New Mexico. Unlike the other two family ranches, the Golden Spur, named after the old gold mine on the property, was being built with Quint's own two hands and from his own ideas and dreams. And that made it all very special to him.

"I heard about your father dying—what was it—two years ago?"

His gaze turned uncomfortably away from her. "Over two years now."

"I was very sorry to hear about Lewis's passing. I met him a couple of times. He was a warm, perfect gentleman."

She saw him swallow and realized that the hurt of losing his father was still a raw wound in him. The vulnerable side of the man touched Maura in a way she'd not expected. She would have liked to place a comforting hand on his shoulder, but to do such a thing would only rouse his suspicions of her. And he did have suspicions, she thought wryly. She'd spotted them in his eyes the moment she'd told him she was living with Abe.

"Yeah. Everyone liked Dad."

Clearing her throat, she replied, "So who's managing the Chaparral now? Obviously, not you."

"Laramie Jones. But I still keep a hand in things there. That's where Mom still makes her home." Eventually, the Chaparral would go to his sister Alexa, and Apache Wells would be split equally between the two siblings. As of now, it was Quint's job to keep an eye on both properties. Not an easy task for Quint, especially since he had his own place to deal with, too. But ranching was his life and he considered the extra work a labor of love.

"I see."

Behind her the coffeemaker gurgled its last drop. Maura walked to the end of the cabinet where the cups were located. "Would you like coffee?" she asked.

"Sure. Thanks."

She gathered up two cups and proceeded to fill both of them. After she'd carried them over to the table and took a seat across from him, she reached for a small pitcher of cream.

As he stirred sugar into his own cup, he said, "This may sound insensitive, but I thought you were married."

Maura tried not to cringe. Being divorced wasn't like she'd committed some sort of shameful crime, but for some reason it bothered her to think this man might be viewing her as a failure. Especially at being a wife, a woman, a lover.

"I was married for five years," she replied. "But it ended more than a year ago. That's when I moved back to Lincoln County."

"Oh."

She pushed a hand through her hair and the thought suddenly struck her that her face was bare of makeup, her hair mussed. But her appearance hardly mattered. This man was at least six years younger. He'd never look at her in a romantic way. Which was more than okay with her. She wasn't ready to tangle herself up in any sort of emotional commitment again. And if she did ever get ready, she would hardly take her chances on a young man who was still in his twenties and apparently not looking to settle down.

"No children?" he asked.

Gripping her cup, she tried to push away the empty ache that always seemed to be lingering near her heart. "No. My ex-husband's job required him to travel all the time. I kept waiting for that to change. It didn't."

She could feel his blue eyes upon her, but she didn't have the courage to lift her gaze to his. "What about you, Mr. Cantrell? You've not married yet?"

He took his time sipping his coffee and as tense moments begin to tick away, Maura decided he was going to ignore her question entirely. Which was embarrassing. Especially since she'd talked about her personal life.

"No," he said finally. "I haven't been looking for a wife. Can't see that I need one."

And why would he? she asked herself. The man had everything. Cattle, horses, thousands of acres of prime ranch land at his disposal, anything that money could buy. And that probably included women; the sort that he could take or leave at his convenience. A young hunk like him probably didn't want to be saddled with a wife.

"And I wish you wouldn't call me Mr. Cantrell," he went on. "That was my father's name. I'm just Quint to everyone."

Calling him Mr. Cantrell helped keep him at an emotional distance. But it looked as though he meant to tear down even that flimsy barrier. Feeling even tenser, she drained her cup and rose to her feet. "Okay, Quint. Will you be staying for supper? There'll be plenty."

He got to his feet and Maura unconsciously stepped backward to put plenty of space between them. He was a big man. In size and presence. Strength and masculinity were stamped all over his rough features, broad shoulders and long, hard legs. Just being near him left her feeling cornered.

"I don't know yet. Right now I'm going to go find my grandfather." He placed his cup in the sink, then went out the back door, the screen banging behind him.

Maura stared after him and wondered why meeting Quint Cantrell had felt like going through an earthquake. Even her hands were still shaking.

Because Jenna Cantrell had wanted the dust and commotion of a ranch yard well away from her home, Abe had built the working part of Apache Wells two miles west of the house. Normally, he and Quint drove the distance, but there were times they chose to walk to the bunkhouse and work pens.

Down through the years, the outbuildings and barns had been built with no particular style or planning in mind, except durability and practical use. Some were made of wood, some corrugated iron, but one thing the buildings did have in common was their whitewashed walls and red tin roofs.

To one side of the network of buildings and connecting holding pens was a long arena where the hands gathered to train their horses to follow and cut cattle, and in quieter times, swap stories around a small campfire.

This late summer evening just happened to be cool enough to appreciate the warmth of a fire and, after Quint parked his truck, he found his grandfather with several of his hired hands squatting around the ring of rocks. The moment Abe spotted his approach, he left the circle of men and walked over to his grandson.

The older man was the same height as Quint and bony thin. He never went outdoors without his black hat and he always wore the legs of his jeans stuffed deep into his knee-high cowboy boots. This particular pair had lime-green tops with fancy yellow stitching and the leather was as scarred and worn as his grandfather's face. Tonight he was wearing a brown quilted vest to ward away the chill and the puffy garment camouflaged his wiry torso.

Stroking his thick white mustache, he said to Quint, "So I see you finally managed to come check on your grandfather."

Not allowing the old man any slack, Quint said, "I had to work at it. But I'm here."

Folding his arms across his chest, Abe rocked back on his high heels. "Well, it's about time." He jerked his head toward the men behind him. "Jim's makin' some camp coffee. Come have a cup with us."

"I just had coffee—with your nurse," Quint added pointedly.

Abe grinned that goofy sort of grin that men got on their faces when they talked about women. "So you met the little filly, did ya? What'd you think about her?"

If Quint hadn't been so shocked at his grandfather's ribald questions, he would have rolled his eyes and cursed a blue streak.

"Forget about that," he muttered. "What the hell are you doing, Gramps? You're not sick! You're using that vertigo problem of yours as an excuse to have her here. Aren't you?"

"S-s-shh! Don't be raising your voice so, damn it! She might hear you."

"*She's* in the house—two miles from here," Quint reasoned.

His head tilting one way and then the other, Abe chuckled. "Well, she thinks I'm needy—and I am. At times. You know, Quint, I always had it in my mind that nurses were hard-hearted women. They sure seem like it when a man is sick. But Maura ain't. She's as sweet as a summer peach."

"Since when did you need a summer peach?" Quint countered.

Abe shrugged. "Well—since I got dizzy."

Quint snorted. "Looks to me like you've gotten more than dizzy."

"That's right," Abe retorted. "I got the notion that I was tired of living alone."

Shaking his head, Quint looked out at the ranch yard. The dipping sun was lengthening the shadows of the buildings. A pen of horses munched on alfalfa while around their feet several dominickers pecked at the morsels of oats and corn that had fallen from the feed troughs. Apache Wells had always felt more like home to Quint than any of the other Cantrell properties in Lincoln County.

As a young child he'd spent many days and nights here with his grandparents and those memories were more than special to him. His time here had influenced his life. The endless days he'd spent with his grandfather working in and out of the saddle had set Quint's goals and visions for the future.

Yes, Apache Wells had always been special to him and he didn't want a woman coming along and changing anything about it.

"Living alone! Gramps, you have men all around you. That's hardly being alone."

"Is that what you tell yourself?" Abe countered with a question.

Quint frowned, then heaved out a heavy breath. "Look, Gramps, I'm not the one complaining about being lonely. You are. My life is one big whirlwind right now. I don't have time to be lonely. And frankly, neither do you. So spare me."

Abe scowled at him. "Spare you? I'd like to kick your ass."

Seeing he was getting nowhere, Quint took a different direction. "So how long do you plan on keeping this nurse?"

Abe gave him a palms-up gesture. "'Til I don't need her, I suppose. 'Course if I get over this dizzy problem, I'm hardly likely to run her off."

Quint suddenly decided he'd been all wrong about the old man. Abe was sick. With dementia or something like it. Had Maura already recognized Abe's problem and saw it as a way to get her foot in the door? He hated to think the woman might be that calculating. She didn't seem the sort, at all. But then, he'd spent four years believing that Holly Johnson was a true-blue innocent and look what that had gotten him. She'd run off with a rich real-estate mogul and Quint had become the laughingstock of Lincoln County.

"Gramps, I want you to have a complete checkup. You need blood work, scans, the whole nine yards. You're not yourself and we both know it."

Abe laughed gleefully. "I'm not acting like myself, am I? Just because I'm enjoying a little female company? I think any doc would say you're the one who's messed up."

"What about Granny?" Quint challenged him. "Doesn't she matter anymore?"

Abe's expression suddenly softened and he patted Quint on the shoulder. "She ain't here anymore, Quint. All I have is memories and photos. A man needs more and you ought to understand that."

Lord, did his grandfather have romantic intentions toward the nurse? "Gramps, did you hire her to be your nurse or something more personal?" Quint asked point-blank.

Abe turned a completely innocent look on him. "Why, to be my nurse, of course. But if she so happens to stumble around and fall in love with me—well, I sure as heck ain't gonna push her away. If you know what I mean."

Unfortunately, Quint knew all too well what his grandfather meant. He also knew that if he didn't do something about this situation and soon, Abe was going to be hurt. In more ways than one.

Gazing thoughtfully in the direction of the ranch house, Quint rubbed a hand against his jaw. "I think I'll stay for supper," he suddenly announced.

Clearly skeptical, Abe asked, "Why? You thinkin'

you're gonna hang around and horn in on your grandfather's business?"

Quint looked at him. "No. I'm thinking that soup she was making smelled mighty good."

He was also thinking that the moment he'd first walked into the kitchen, Maura Donovan had set off some sort of spark in him, a flash of heat that had taken Quint totally by surprise. Now he wanted to get closer to the woman, he decided. So close that he could see right into her pretty head. He could take a second look into her green eyes and found out for himself if that spark he'd felt had been real or imagined.

Though he wasn't too sure which direction he wanted the decision to land...

# Chapter Two

Two days later, on the dirt drive that led to the Apache Wells ranch house, Maura was finishing the last of a two-mile jog. The early afternoon sun was hot. Sweat sheened her body and dampened her red tank top. The thought of languishing over a tall glass of iced tea pushed her forward, until the musical ring of her cell phone sounded in the pocket of her shorts.

Pausing in the middle of the narrow road, she fished out the small instrument and was immediately surprised to see the caller was her mother. Now that the Donovan children were all grown and capable of running the Diamond D horse ranch without them, her parents, Fiona and Doyle Donovan, had become regular globe-trotters. Only two days ago they'd been in Ireland visiting relatives on both sides of their extensive families.

"Hello, Mother!"

"You're out of breath," Fiona observed. "What did you do, run to the phone?"

"No. I'm out jogging," Maura explained.

"Oh. I can call back later."

Having five siblings meant that getting any exclusive, one-on-one attention from their mother was rare and precious. Just having her mother call so quickly after her return home made Maura feel special.

"Nonsense. I can walk and talk for a while," she assured the other woman. "It's so good to hear your voice. When did you get home?"

"Late last night. Your father and I are so jet-lagged we're just getting around to having breakfast. Dallas was the only one still up when we arrived last night and this afternoon everyone seems to be out of pocket."

"Just because you and Dad live the life of luxury doesn't mean your children can loll around in bed until midafternoon," Maura teased as she started to the house.

"Hmm. It's good to hear that we've taught you children good work ethics. And speaking of work, Dallas tells me you're still with Mr. Cantrell."

Before her parents had left for Ireland more than a month ago, Abe had not yet approached Maura about the job here at Apache Wells. But once she'd decided to take the old man's offer, she'd called her parents in Ireland and told them about her decision. Neither had understood her choice to abruptly change jobs, but they'd hardly tried to deter her. At thirty-six, it had been years since her parents had tried to tell her what to do. And even if they did try, Maura was too stubborn and strong-minded not to take the path she chose for herself. Even if it might be the wrong path, she thought drily.

"That's right."

"So what are your duties? Does he keep you busy fetching and complaining?"

Maura smiled to herself. "Not in the least. Right now Abe is out riding range with the rest of the ranch hands. I don't expect him in until later this afternoon."

"Riding—" Fiona gasped. "I thought—if I remember correctly, Abe Cantrell is older than your father! And I thought he was ill and needed a nurse!"

The smile on Maura's full lips deepened even more. "Abe is eighty-four. And he's as healthy as a horse. Except for when he gets vertigo. And thankfully that's only happened once since I've been here."

There was a long pause and then Fiona said in a slow, pointed voice, "Maura, I may be butting in, but I'd like to know why you gave up a wonderful, good-paying job at the hospital for a man who only needs you occasionally?"

"Abe needs me more than occasionally, Mother."

"You just assured me he was healthy and—"

"He needs me in other, emotional ways. Having me here makes him feel secure. Besides that, he's lonely and starved for affection."

"Maura!" Fiona said in a scolding tone. "You hardly know this man. His emotional needs aren't your responsibility."

Maura had told herself exactly that same thing. More than once. Yet for some reason she couldn't explain to anyone, a part of her had connected to the old man the minute she'd first met him striding down a hallway at Sierra General. He'd been trying to find his way through the maze of corridors to the closest exit and Maura had offered her help. The two of them had hit it off instantly and before Abe had left the building, he'd offered her the private nursing job.

"Mother, I'm a nurse and Abe needs mental and physical nourishing. That's what my job is all about," Maura responded. "The degree of his need has nothing to do with things."

On the other end of the line, she could hear her mother sighing softly. "You've gotten attached to this man. I can hear it in your voice," Fiona said flatly.

"I suppose I have."

"And what about Frankie, his daughter-in-law? And his grandson—what is his name?"

"Quint."

"Yes, Quint. What about them, aren't they around to see to Abe's needs?"

Maura talked to Frankie on a frequent basis and the woman had made it clear that even though she checked in on Abe from time to time, Quint was the one relative the old man wanted and needed in his life. Frankie had also assured her that she was going to keep mum about Maura and let Abe be the one to tell his grandson about having a nurse. Obviously Frankie had kept her word. Two days ago, when he'd appeared unannounced in the kitchen, he'd been shocked to find Maura there and she'd been totally tilted off-kilter by his presence. Since then it had been impossible to forget the strong physical reaction she'd felt toward the man. Just thinking about him made her feel utterly foolish.

"The Cantrells are busy people. Just like you and Dad. They have lives of their own to deal with."

In fact, the night Quint had sat down to eat supper with her and Abe, he'd received some sort of important call and hadn't even taken the time to gulp more than three bites before he'd quickly departed the ranch. Abe had clearly been disappointed when his grandson had rushed off. As for Maura, she'd felt deflated as she'd watched the man dash out the door. A part of her had wanted more of his company while the other part had been leery of the strange feelings he'd elicited in her.

"I'm sorry if I sounded fussy, darling," Fiona said after a pause. "If you like the job, that's all that matters. But I can't see why you'd want to isolate yourself out there on Apache Wells, though. It's miles and miles from anything."

Because the isolation was soothing to her fractured nerves, Maura thought. Because after going through a humiliating, heartbreaking divorce, not to mention the unwanted chase by Dr. Weston, Maura needed the calm quiet of Abe's home to restore herself.

"My truck is in good working order and I can drive into town whenever I want. I promise to see you and Dad soon."

"I'm holding you to that promise and—"

Fiona broke off as Maura caught the sound of her father's voice booming in the background for his wife to hang up the phone and come to breakfast.

"You'd better put the phone down, Mother. Dad never did like waiting on his meals."

Laughing, Fiona said goodbye and quickly closed the connection between them. Maura put her own phone back in her pocket and trotted on to the house.

She was nearing the porch when the screen door pushed open and Abe stepped onto the small alcove.

"There you are!" he exclaimed. "I've been huntin' all over for you."

"I've been out getting a little exercise," Maura said with a smile. "Did everything go okay on your ride? Any dizziness?"

He grinned at her and Maura thought that it must be true that the older a man got the more he resembled the boy he'd once been. Abe was one of the most mischievous, prank-playing men she'd ever been around and that included her three rowdy brothers.

"Not even one little spin. Everything went as fine as spring rain. Got the cattle moved and the old pump off the broken windmill. We'll have it fixed in a few days."

Maura gestured toward one of the two lawn chairs grouped together on the small porch. "Sit down and I'll get you coffee or something," she suggested.

"Don't have time. We got some green colts penned and some of the boys are gonna try to halter 'em. I'd better be there. These young'ns try to hurry things along. I have a hell of a time tryin' to teach them that when you're dealin' with horses, the slow way is the fastest way."

Maura smiled. How many times had she heard her own father say the same thing, she wondered fondly. Like Abe, Doyle Donovan was a horseman and would be until he died.

Turning toward the house, Abe motioned for her to follow. "Come along inside," Abe said to her. "I've got a chore for ya. That is, if you don't mind doin' it."

Curious, Maura followed the old man into the house, where he immediately walked over to a rolltop desk that was situated in one corner of the small living room. Inside the desk, he pulled a large white envelope from one of the storage slots, then waved it in Maura's face.

"This came in the mail yesterday. Quint needs to look it over. Pronto. I called him last night, but he says he can't get back over here for a few days. I'd like for you to take these papers over to the Golden Spur."

Go to Quint Cantrell's ranch? The thought of seeing the

man again sent a thrill of excitement zinging through Maura. Yet at the same time, she was wary of meeting him on her own without Abe's presence to act as a buffer. The other evening, during his short visit, Quint had been polite enough to her, yet she'd sensed he wasn't all that pleased about Abe's having a nurse. If he decided to really jump her out about the issue, she didn't know how she would handle him.

*Lord, Maura, you wouldn't know how to handle Quint Cantrell under any circumstance. He's way too much man for a woman like you. And don't you forget it.*

"I—well, if it's important to you, I'd be glad to," she finally said. After all, the man was paying her an extravagant wage for being his private nurse. And it was her job to see that he didn't fret unduly over things. "Is the ranch hard to find?"

"No trouble at all," he said with a dismissive wave of his hand. "I'll make you a little map while you go fix yourself up or whatever it is you women do before you leave the house."

Maura wasn't about to fix herself up for Quint Cantrell, but she couldn't say that to Abe. Instead she went to her room and hurriedly showered, then changed into a cool white shirt over a pair of Levi's. After swiping a brush through her hair and a bit of peach color across her lips, she returned to the living room and found Abe waiting with the map and papers in hand.

As he watched her approach, a wide grin spread across his face. "Here you go, honey. The map is easy to follow. Just take your time and don't get in no hurry to get back here. I feel good. Not nary a vertigo spell. Maybe I'm plumb over 'em."

Abe's way of putting things made Maura want to laugh

out loud. Instead, she said with a straight face, "If you're plumb over them, Abe, then you probably don't need me to keep hanging around here."

Frowning now, he reached out a bony hand to grip one of her shoulders. "Maura, now I was just tryin' to be positive. We both know that those damned spells could hit me right out of the blue. And I ain't lyin' when I say that they're scary things. Makes me feel like I'm dyin'. What would I do if you weren't around to get my head straight and all those little marbles back in place?"

He had ten men working here on this end of the ranch, not to mention several more on the western half of Apache Wells property. Except for the nights, the man was never alone. True, none of the ranch hands had any medical training, but then Abe wasn't looking for them or her to keep him physically safe, she realized. It was becoming obvious to her that he wanted her here for other, emotional reasons, and for now Maura was content to leave things at that.

"They're not marbles that make you dizzy, they're pieces of calcium that float around," she pointed out to him. "But don't worry, Abe. I'm not leaving. I just want to make sure that you're still okay with me being here."

The worried frown on his face eased into a genuine smile. "I'm better than okay. Havin' you around is almost like havin' Jenna back."

Maura patted his arm. Since she'd moved onto the ranch, Abe had talked to her a lot about his late wife. He was clearly still in love with the woman and missed her greatly. She empathized with the old man's loss. Especially now that she was on her own and her bed was as empty as her heart.

"I'm glad," she said softly, then clearing her throat, she promised, "I'll be back later this evening."

An hour later, on Highway 380, Maura very nearly missed the small sign on the left side of the road. *Golden Spur* were the only words written on the piece of tin nailed to a cedar fence post, but that was enough to tell Maura it was Cantrell property. The simple sign also told her that there was nothing showy about Quint Cantrell.

Turning into the entrance, she drove her Ford over the wooden cattle guard, then pulled to one side of the dusty road to study the map Abe had sketched for her.

From this point she would travel north for ten miles, then take the left fork in the road and drive due west for five more miles. The ranch house, Abe had told her, sat at the foot of a bald mountain.

Before she could take note of the butterflies in her stomach, Maura lifted her chin and stepped down on the gas. There wasn't any need for her nerves to jump around like a swarm of grasshoppers, she assured herself. It wasn't like she was going to see the man for personal reasons. All she was doing was making a delivery.

Normally, Quint was rarely in the house during the daytime. He couldn't waste the daylight. But today the wire stretchers had malfunctioned and barbed wire had popped loose, lashing backward to catch Quint's forearm. The long barbs had ripped the denim fabric of his shirt like a piece of fragile paper and torn a deep gash into his flesh.

The bleeding had forced him to come to the house and make an effort to patch up the wound. Now as he stood at the bathroom sink, pouring alcohol into the angry lesion and gritting his teeth against the sting, he heard a faint knock at the front door.

Figuring it was the man he'd been working with, he

yelled out, "Come on in, Jake. Get yourself a beer from the fridge, while I try to wrap up this thing."

"Um—this isn't Jake," a female voice called back.

Stunned by the sound, Quint wrapped a small towel around the wounded arm and hurried out of the bathroom and down a short hallway to the living room. The moment he spotted Maura standing just inside the door, he halted in his tracks.

"What are you doing here?" he asked without preamble.

She answered his question by holding up a long white envelope. "The papers your grandfather wanted you to have. He sent me to deliver them."

Papers? Quint couldn't remember talking to his grandfather about papers, but then his days and nights were filled with so many tasks that after a while everything began to run together. Besides, he could hardly think. Just seeing Maura Donovan standing inside the walls of his house was enough to jar his senses. Dressed in a pair of clinging jeans and a close-fitting shirt, she was just as sexy and attractive as he remembered and for a few seconds he forgot about the pain slicing through his arm.

"Oh. Well, just lay them anywhere, would you? Right now I'm—" Grimacing he glanced ruefully down at his arm. "I'm in a bit of a mess. If you'll excuse me, I'll—"

Her eyes followed his gaze down to the bloody towel wrapped around his arm. Quickly stepping forward, she exclaimed, "You've hurt yourself! Let me help."

Quint unconsciously took a step backward. "It's not that bad. Just give me a minute and I'll slap a bandage on it."

Concern marking her brow, Maura placed the envelope on the nearest end table, then closed the distance between them. "Don't be silly, Quint. I'm a nurse." Not waiting for his permission, she wrapped her hand firmly around his upper arm. "It's my job to deal with wounds."

Since Quint could hardly argue that point, especially now that she had a grip on him, he said, "Okay. I have some things set out in the bathroom. Let's go in there."

Dropping her hold on his arm, she followed him down a short hallway and into the small room. A vanity surrounded a white lavatory and after he'd removed the towel and his shirt, she quickly positioned his injured limb over the clean basin.

"How did this happen?" she asked.

"A piece of barbed wire came loose from the stretcher and whacked me."

She was taller than he'd first thought, he realized. If her head hadn't been bent over his arm, the top of it would have measured to a spot just beneath chin.

"It looks to me as though this could use a stitch or two," she told him. "Have you had a tetanus shot lately?"

The close proximity of her body was rattling him, while the sweet, flowery scent of her skin and hair seemed foreign to a man that mostly kept his distance from women.

"No," he answered gruffly. "Just clean the thing out and I'll take my chances."

Turning her head, she gave him an impatient glance. "That's not very smart of you."

"I've never been accused of being smart. Besides, you medical people go overboard with precautionary measures. Gramps would consider this a scratch."

A soft sigh escaped her. "Have you always tried to fashion yourself after your grandfather?"

"Not always." Quint certainly wouldn't have a nurse living with him, he thought ruefully. Especially if he didn't need one.

Thankfully, she turned her attention back to his arm and Quint gritted his teeth as she used a nail brush to scrub the lesion with water and antibacterial soap.

"What the hell are you doing?" he demanded. "Trying to rip open my arm even more?"

"Sorry. I know it hurts, but it's important to make sure no debris is left behind. Was the wire rusty?"

"No. It was new—galvanized." To his surprise the scrubbing hadn't made the bleeding worse. In fact, it was on the verge of stopping completely.

"That's good," she said. "At least we don't have that problem to worry about."

We? It was his arm. As far as he could see, she didn't have anything to worry about. But he kept the thought to himself. If she was kind enough to offer her services, he could at least show his gratitude.

Once she had the cut clean and dried, she applied antiseptic, then ointment. Quint couldn't help but notice how her hands had gentled during the process and now her fingers felt warm and soothing against his flesh as she slowly wrapped gauze around his forearm.

"Is this all the gauze you have?" she asked.

"Afraid so. I might have some horse bandage down at the barn," he suggested.

She glanced up at him and Quint felt something inside him jerk as he met her earthy-green gaze. There was something very womanly about Maura Donovan, something he couldn't ignore, but was desperately trying to.

"No thanks," she replied. "I'll make do."

Her focus returned to his arm and Quint found himself taking in her dark hair. It was smooth and shiny and threaded with lighter and darker shades that all blended to make an auburn shade so deep it verged on being black.

The length of it nearly reached her waist and Quint wondered how it would look draped against her naked back.

"There. That should keep it protected for a while," she announced as she rose to her full height. "But I wouldn't advise getting the bandage wet and you'll have to change it tomorrow or the next day."

To Quint's dismay, he realized he'd only caught a portion of her words because his mind had been too busy conjuring erotic images of her. What was the matter with him? Since Holly had dumped him for another man, he'd found it damned easy to ignore the sexual pull of a woman. The humiliation she'd put him through had killed his libido deader than a dose of potassium nitrate.

But now, with this sultry nurse standing far too close for his comfort, he was feeling things again. Things that could only lead to trouble.

"I'll be sure to take good care of it."

She slowly released her hold on him, then turned to fetch his shirt from the end of the vanity. When she pivoted back, she was holding the shirt out for him to stick his arms through.

"Let me have it," he said. "I don't need help getting dressed."

"Don't try to act like such a he-man," she said softly. "I won't tell anybody I helped you."

Knowing it wasn't wise to linger in such close quarters with her, he decided not to argue and was glad that he hadn't as he struggled to push the bundled arm through the shirtsleeve.

"Don't be surprised if your arm is already starting to feel stiff," she said. "You're going to have one hell of a sore muscle for a while."

"I'm finding that out," Quint muttered.

Once his arms were in the sleeves, she smoothed the fabric over his shoulders, then stepped back to allow him to button the garment himself. Quint found it safer to look at the buttons rather than her.

"A couple of over-the-counter pain relievers will help."

"I have some in the kitchen," he told her, then motioned for her to precede him out the door. "Would you like something cool to drink? It's the least I can do for bandaging me. I was having a heck of a time trying to manage with one hand."

He began to move down a short hallway and Maura followed him into a large kitchen. A row of paned windows ran along the west wall of the room and without any curtains or shades to cover them, the afternoon sun streamed golden shafts across the old printed linoleum covering the floor.

The house was very livable, yet it was far from fancy. In fact, Maura was totally surprised to see how modest Quint's living quarters actually were. Anyone who'd lived for any length of time in Lincoln County and beyond was aware that the Cantrell family was rich. Abe owned thousands and thousands of acres and his cattle ranch, Apache Wells, had long been one of the most profitable in the state. On another section of land, just north of Alto, Quint's father, Lewis, had also built a cattle empire called the Chaparral. Maura had never visited that particular ranch, but her parents and older brother Conall had attended a party there. From what they'd said, the Chaparral house was a showy hacienda with luxury and space to spare. So why was the younger Cantrell living like this? she wondered. Because he wanted to emulate his grandfather?

While he headed to the refrigerator, he gestured toward

a small, round dining table. "Have a seat," he invited. "I have beer, soda or fruit juice. Take your pick."

"Soda is fine," she told him as she eased onto one of the wooden chairs.

He carried two chilled cans of cola over to the table and pushed one her way, but didn't immediately take a seat. Instead, he walked over to a row of cabinets, fished out a bottle of acetaminophen and shook two out in the palm of his hand.

"I'm glad to see you're going to take my advice," she said as she popped the lid on her drink.

He tossed the pills into his mouth and washed them down with a long drink of the soda before he walked over to the table and took a seat across from her.

"I still have a stretch of fence to finish before it gets dark," he explained. "I don't want my arm to get too stiff to work."

There was no way he needed to be straining his arm using post-hole diggers or wire stretchers, but she wasn't going to bother pointing that out to him. He was a grown man and his well-being was not her responsibility. Besides, being a nurse had taught her that there wasn't a man alive who wanted a woman to hamper him with limitations.

"So this is where you've been doing all this work that Abe talks about," she commented. "As I drove up I noticed the new barn. It looks nice."

"Thanks. The barn is taking a lot more work and twice as much money as I'd first anticipated. But I think it's turning out okay."

He must have removed his hat when he'd come into the house to attend his cut, she thought. It was only the second time she'd seen him without the battered felt atop his head.

The other being when he'd sat down at Abe's dinner table. But that occasion hadn't lasted long enough for him to get the chair warm. Now, as quiet moments ticked by, she couldn't help but notice the thick, rusty wave dipped across one corner of his forehead, the unruly strands curling around his ears.

His face and arms were tanned as dark as a coffee bean, but the glimpses she'd had of his bare chest told her he wasn't into lounging around in the sun without his shirt. She doubted he was into lounging around anywhere. From the looks of his lean, hard muscles, the man worked tirelessly.

Her carnal thoughts brought her up short. The two of them were entirely alone and with the letter delivered and his arm bandaged, she no longer had any good reason to remain in Quint Cantrell's house.

Quickly rising to her feet, she said nervously, "Well, I'm glad that I didn't interrupt your work—though I guess the injury to your arm had already done that. But I won't keep you any longer. I promised Abe I'd be back to Apache Wells before it got too late."

Quint rose to his feet also. "You haven't finished your soda."

"I've had enough. Thank you."

She started out of the kitchen and as she did, she could feel Quint's presence following close behind her. The idea made her heart thump at a rapid pace and she drew in a deep breath in an attempt to calm it.

"I'm not in that big of a hurry to get back to work, Maura. Why don't you let me show you around before you leave?"

His suggestion caught her by surprise and she dared to glance over her shoulder at him. "Do you really want to?"

He suddenly chuckled and Maura was amazed at how different he looked with humor softening his features.

"I don't make offers unless I want to."

Something about the husky tone of his voice, the warmth in his eyes, sent prickles of excitement racing through her. She could feel her cheeks growing warm and pink and she suddenly felt like a foolish teenager instead of a thirty-six-year-old woman who'd been married and divorced.

But just for this once, she wasn't going to think about the dangers this man represented to her peace of mind. Tomorrow she would remind herself that she was behaving like an idiot. Today she was going to let herself enjoy the pleasure of being in the presence of a very sexy man.

"In that case," she said, "I'd love to have a look around."

Moving forward, he touched a hand to her back and Maura felt her senses splintering in all directions.

"Good," he murmured. "Just let me get my hat and we'll be on our way," he told her.

## Chapter Three

Once they stepped onto the porch, Quint dropped his hand from her back and Maura was finally able to draw in a normal breath. But as they moved into the yard, he immediately wrapped a hold around her upper arm.

"Let's go to the barn first," he suggested. "I need to let Jake, my ranch hand, know I'm okay."

Nodding, she looked away from him and tried not to dwell on his warm, rough fingers pressing into her flesh.

The afternoon was all bright sunshine, while a soft west wind carried the scent of sagebrush and juniper. A lone aspen shaded one corner of the house, but that was the only bona fide tree that she could see for miles around. The rest of the vegetation growing beyond the ranch yard amounted to a few spindly pinyon pines, some twisted snags of juniper and a sea of jumping choya cactus and sagebrush. It was a stark, yet beautiful sight and Maura instinctively knew it would be even more so in the late evening when the sun fell from the sky and twilight purpled the nearby mountains.

"How many men do you have working for you?" she asked.

Now that they were walking abreast, he dropped his hold on her arm and Maura didn't know whether to be disappointed or relieved. Either way, just being this near him left her shaky and nothing like the practical, no-nonsense nurse that had dealt calmly with all sorts of men. She kept remembering the way he'd looked without his shirt and how the warmth and scent of his body had filled up the little bathroom and stifled her breath.

"The contractor working on the barn and storage sheds has several men working with him. But as far as the ranch goes, I only have two hands. Once I start putting livestock on the place, I'll hire more. Though my grandfather deeded over the land a few years ago, I only started full-time here about two years ago."

She kept her gaze on the rocky ground in front of her. "Do you have plenty of land here to support cattle?"

"Ten thousand acres. Not that much, but enough to do what I want to do."

Glancing over at him, she asked curiously, "And what is that?"

He shrugged and not for the first time, Maura couldn't help thinking how serious and driven he was for a man his age. Abe had commented one day that his grandson wasn't yet thirty so that meant he was either twenty-eight or twenty-nine. He certainly didn't look any older than that, Maura thought. Yet he seemed older, as though the years he'd been on this earth had pushed his soul to manhood long before his body had caught up.

"My plans aren't anything grand. Just raise a few pure-bred cattle and a few horses."

"What about the old gold mine—the Golden Spur—that your ranch is named after?"

She'd not meant to ask that question. It had just slipped out on its own. The same way her heart seemed to jump into a crazy jig each time she looked at his face.

Frowning, he glanced her way. "What about it?" he asked curtly.

Knowing she'd touched on a tender spot, she shrugged in an effort to appear casual. "Nothing really. Except that I couldn't help noticing the letter Abe asked me to deliver to you. The return address was Red Bluff Mining Company. And your grandfather doesn't make any secret about wanting to reopen the old thing."

His footsteps paused on the barren ground and Maura came to a stop with him. As he looked at her, she could see frustration edging his features.

"Gramps thinks the mine could be profitable again. But I don't want anything to do with it. Having a bunch of trucks and men and equipment going across the ranch is the last thing I need."

"If it turned out to be profitable, the extra money might come in handy," she suggested. "Especially when you start buying stock for this place."

"I don't need the money," he said flatly. "Nor do I want it. I'm a rancher, not a miner."

He picked up his stride again, only this time it was much longer and purposeful as he covered the last few yards to the barn. Maura quickened her steps to stay up with him.

"So if money isn't the issue, why does your grandfather want to reopen the mine?" she said, darting a quick glance at his sober face.

"For the adventure, Maura. He's always wanted to turn over a rock just to see what was beneath it. That's how he got rich in the first place—on the plains of Texas, drilling for oil. He hit it big and brought his fortune out here to New Mexico to buy land and cattle. To him, the mine takes him back to those days when he was drilling for black gold. Guess it makes him feel young all over again. He didn't care about the mine for years when he owned it, but now that I have the land, it's all he seems to care about."

"Sometimes feeling young or having a dream is very important. Sometimes it even keeps a person from dying."

The muscles around his hard mouth tightened with impatience. "Don't try to make me believe that Gramps is dying. That he needs you or the mine to keep him healthy."

"I wouldn't attempt such a thing," she said defensively. "Abe isn't ill. He has a perfectly good mind. And the way I see it, he has the right to dream his own dreams. Just like you."

By now they had reached the massive barn. Instead of opening the huge double doors at the south end of the building, Quint led her to a smaller entrance at the side.

With his hand pausing on the door latch, he turned a searching look on her. "And what about you, Maura? What are your dreams?"

A few years ago his questions would have been easy to answer. Her dreams were waiting for the day her roving husband would settle down to a life exclusively with her. She'd been dreaming of the time they could start having children and Gilbert would be home so that they could parent them together. She'd waited because he kept promising he'd be ready the next year, and she wanted to raise her children with her husband home every night. But none of those dreams had come true. Instead, she'd discovered he'd changed women as often as he'd changed the cities his job had taken him to. And she'd had to accept the fact of his infidelity and that he'd never intended to change his job and settle down to family life. That had only been one of his false promises.

Maura had spent the past year trying to restore her broken self-confidence and move on from her shattered marriage. For months after her divorce, she'd struggled to simply put one foot in front of the other, and looking back, she realized her responsibilities as a nurse had been the only thing keeping her going. She was good at her job and no man could take that fact away from her. As for her dreams, she wasn't sure what they were now.

"I don't know, Quint," she said honestly. "Sometimes dreams get lost along the way."

Nobody had to tell him that, he thought grimly. His romantic dreams had been busted years ago. Now his goals were concrete and didn't depend on another person—particularly a woman.

"Yeah," he murmured. "And when that happens, it's damned hard to find new ones."

While the two of them had been talking, her face had taken on a sad hue and Quint realized he didn't like seeing her in such a mood. Maybe because it reminded him of his own lonely existence. Or maybe because he simply didn't like to think of this woman suffering over anyone or anything.

The unwanted notions disturbed him so much that he quickly turned away from her and shoved open the door.

"Let's go in," he urged. "I think Jake is probably at the back of the building where the men are working."

Since livestock hadn't yet been moved onto the ranch, the barn was missing the smells of animals and hay and leather. Instead, the scents of sawdust and fresh paint filled the air. On the opposite side of the building, a table saw buzzed and hammers rang out as men erected a frame of lumber that Quint explained would eventually become a large feed room.

"The contractor hasn't yet finished the horse stalls or the tack room. They'll get to that next," Quint continued as they slowly made their way through the building.

She was looking around her with real interest, a fact that surprised Quint. Even though she came from a ranching background, she didn't seem the sort that would be personally interested in such things. After all, she'd chosen a profession outside the Diamond D, her family's famous thoroughbred ranch. Add to that, she had a soft, feminine air about her that was totally opposite of an outdoor girl.

"This is going to be very nice," she said. "And I like the way you've laid out everything. When you open the big doors, the horses will be able to look outside. They like that, you know. When they can see what's going on, they're more content."

Bemused by her observation, Quint paused to look at her. Now that they were indoors, her features were muted by shadows, yet the dimness couldn't diminish the pearly sheen of her skin and for a brief moment he wondered what it would feel like to press his cheek against hers, to experience such softness next to him.

"You know about horses, do you?" he asked.

A smile tilted her lips and at that moment he decided he'd never seen anything so fetching or genuine.

"Why wouldn't I? My family raises thoroughbreds."

He folded his arms against his chest. "But you don't work with them. The horses, I mean."

Her smile turned whimsical. "No. Not since I went

into nursing. But I spent a lot of time at the barns when I was young."

"I know that Bridget is a doctor, but if I remember correctly, you have another sister. What does she do?"

She glanced away from him. "Dallas operates Angel Wing Stables, a therapy riding clinic for handicapped children. It's completely nonprofit and something she feels deeply about."

So all three of the Donovan sisters were dedicated to helping needy people. That should have reassured Quint and allowed him to quit worrying about Abe hiring Maura as his nurse. But it didn't. The more he got to know this woman, the more concerned he was. And not because he believed she was out to snag any sort of money from the old man. No, he'd written that idea off fairly quickly. The more he'd thought about it, the more he'd concluded she wasn't the gold-digger sort. Furthermore, the Donovans had just as much money or more than the Cantrells. She didn't need it.

No, Quint was far more concerned about his grandfather's emotional state than his bank account. It was obvious the old man had already grown extremely fond of Maura. And just because Abe was in his eighties, didn't mean he was immune to a female's charms. His grandfather might even fall in love with her. Stranger things had happened. And Maura had just now talked about the importance of a man's dreams. When she left Apache Wells, and she would, what would happen to his grandfather's dreams? They'd be broken.

Forcing his thoughts back to the moment, he touched a hand to her shoulder and urged her forward. "I see Jake. Let's go catch up with him."

At the end of the building, a young man wearing a black cowboy hat and ranch gear was applying neat's-foot oil to a fancy tooled saddle. The moment he saw their approach, he laid the oily rag to one side and stepped up to meet them.

"I was about to come to the house to make sure you weren't bleeding to death," he said to Quint, while his gaze strayed curiously over to Maura.

"I'm fine," Quint replied. "It just so happens that Maura is a nurse. She was kind enough to bandage me up."

A wry grin crossed the man's face. "Now isn't that something? A beautiful woman comes to your house and she's a nurse—just when you need one. You always were a lucky dog, Quint."

Quint couldn't see where slicing his arm open was lucky, but apparently Jake considered having Maura as a nurse more than fortunate. The idea grated on Quint to no end. Which was a ridiculous reaction. She wasn't anything to him. If Jake, or any man, wanted to make a play for her, then that was their business, not his.

"Maura, this is my good friend and ranch hand, Jake Rollins. Jake, this is Maura Donovan. She's my grandfather's personal nurse."

Ignoring the last tidbit, the dark-haired man reached to take Maura's hand. "Are you by any chance related to Liam Donovan?" he asked.

She smiled at Jake and Quint had to fight the urge to jerk her away from the other man and usher her back outside where the two of them would be alone, where her smiles would be directed only at him.

What the hell was coming over him? Quint wondered with self-disgust. Instead of worrying about his grandfather, he needed to be concerned about his own reaction to this woman. He was behaving like a moony bull turned loose in a herd of cows.

"He's my brother," Maura said.

"I know him from working the barns at Ruidoso Downs," Jake informed her. "Nice guy. Heck of a trainer, too. No one told me that he had a beautiful sister."

Quint made a loud display of clearing his throat. "You'd better finish that saddle, Jake. In a few minutes, we've got to get back on that wire stretcher."

The other man cast him a look of faint surprise, then reluctantly dropped Maura's hand. "Maybe you'd better keep Maura around. Just in case one of us gets hurt again," he joked. "Next time it might be me who needs her touch."

"Keep it up, Jake, and I'll make sure you get tangled up in barbed wire," Quint muttered, then carefully steered Maura away from the ranch hand and out a back door.

Once they were well away from the barn, Maura asked, "Have you two known each other long?"

Quint grimaced. "Since kindergarten. We grew up together. He's like a brother. That's why I put up with his big mouth."

Smiling, Maura shrugged. "I didn't pay him any mind. He was only joking."

"Don't bet on it. Jake loves women. Always has."

They were walking toward a long corral built of rough cedar boards. Attached to one end were several smaller pens with separate gates leading to the outside. Like the barn, the riding arena would have taken lots of time and effort to build. And as Maura looked around her, she could plainly see that Quint was far from the idle sort. He obviously worked hard for everything he had and she admired him greatly for that. Especially when she knew he loved what he was doing.

Gilbert, her ex-husband, had been a pharmaceutical representative and his job was to sell medical products to doctors in private practices, health clinics and hospitals. There was nothing physical about the job. He'd used his mouth and a pen. Two things he was good at. Especially the mouth, she thought grimly. He could sweet-talk a rabid dog into lying down and wagging its tail.

Thanks to his glib tongue, everyone had liked Gil and for several years running, he'd been top salesperson for his company. And that same gift of gab had made him very attractive to women, including Maura. In the beginning of their marriage his sweet talk had sustained and convinced her of his love. Then later, when things between them had grown difficult and doubts of his sincerity had haunted her, that same sweet, persuasive talk had kept her clinging to a man who was incapable of changing.

Yes, she knew all about flirts and all about trying to keep a man at her side. The first had fooled her into thinking she could succeed at the second. And in the end, her five-year marriage had crumbled along with her self-worth.

Shaking away the humiliating thoughts, Maura leaned a shoulder against the board fence and gazed back at the simple stucco house. What would it be like, she wondered, to live in such a simple place? With Quint Cantrell? He wasn't a wanderer. Apparently he was a homebody, choosing to make his livelihood, his future, with the land. But it didn't appear that he was a family man. Or maybe he was and just keeping those plans hidden, she silently mused.

"You're going to have a fine place to raise a family here someday, Quint."

His features stiffened. "It'll raise cattle and horses. As for a family—I'm not looking for a woman or family right now," he said flatly. "And I'm sure not holding my breath until that day."

Seeing that her comment had rubbed him the wrong way, she pushed away from the fence. "Well, thanks for the tour, Quint. I enjoyed it. But I'd better be heading back. It's not exactly a short drive back to Apache Wells."

She started walking back in the direction of the house and her parked truck. Quint followed alongside her.

"Gramps rarely leaves Apache Wells. Maybe you can talk him into coming over here and taking a look at all the work we've finished. If that doesn't interest him, then maybe visiting the old mine might budge him."

Just from his words, Maura could see that having his grandfather's admiration meant a lot to him. But what else really mattered to this man? If there was no special woman, no children to be had in his dreams, then what was the Golden Spur going to mean to him? Other than just a place to hang his hat?

*At least the man has a future planned for himself, Maura. You have nothing on your agenda, except taking care of an old cantankerous man who could buy a dozen nurses like yourself.*

Shoving away the mocking voice in her head, she said to Quint, "I'll see what I can do about getting him to come for a visit. But I'm sure I don't have to tell you that your grandfather does what he wants. Not what others would like for him to do."

"No. You don't have to tell me that."

As they walked the remaining distance to the house, Quint realized he couldn't keep his eyes off the woman. Her white shirt was sheer enough for him to see the imprint of her bra, the pattern of feminine lace covering her breasts.

She was not a small woman and he could tell by the silhouette of her curves that one breast would be more than enough to fill his hand, his mouth. The idea caused desire to flicker in some part of him that he'd long ago crossed off as dead. And he could only wonder what it was about her that had suddenly stirred him like this.

Since Holly had removed herself from his life, and he'd gotten burned by some superficial gold diggers, sex had become casual, something to forget afterward. And down through the years he'd pushed so hard and so long that he'd felt positive he'd never want another woman in his lifetime.

So why had Maura Donovan come along and reminded him that he was still a man? Lord, he didn't know the answer. But now that she had, he was going to have to deal with her and himself in a smart and practical way.

At the truck, Quint opened the driver's door and helped her up into the cab. She smiled down at him and he felt his practicality fly off with the dusty wind.

"Thank you for taking care of my cut," he said.

"You're welcome. Although, I wish you would consider going to a doctor. With a stitch or two, you would heal even quicker. And depending on how long it's been since you've had one, you might need a tetanus shot."

His lips took on a wry slant. "If I ran into town and got a tetanus shot every time I cut or punctured myself, I'd need a new set of tires every few weeks. Not to mention my body would look like a pincushion," he said, then added in a more serious tone, "But I promise I had a booster a little while ago."

Her smile turned to one of patient resignation. "Okay, I guess I trust you to take care of yourself." She turned her attention to starting the engine, then glanced back at him. "Goodbye, Quint."

He lifted a hand in farewell and she quickly backed

away from him, then headed the nose of her truck down the rocky drive.

The urge to watch her drive away clawed at Quint, but he forced himself to turn in the direction of the barn. Her unexpected visit was over, he told himself. More than likely she wouldn't return to the Golden Spur. And that was for the best.

The Diamond D thoroughbred ranch was located in a stretch of valley known as the Hondo Valley, a rich, fertile area where ranchers raised cattle and horses, and farmers tended acres of fruit orchards. To the north and south of the Donovan ranch house, desert mountains jutted starkly toward the sky, while in-between, irrigated meadows grew seas of knee-deep grass. The three-mile graveled track leading to the house split through one of those lush meadows and Maura drove slowly as she watched a herd of mares frolic with their colts behind a white board fence. Closer to the road, tall Lombardy poplars edged the long drive and towered like green spires into a sky as blue as Quint Cantrell's eyes.

A rueful grimace touched Maura's mouth as she steered her truck to a stop in front of the huge house built of native rock trimmed with rough cedar. She'd driven to the Diamond D this afternoon for a quick hello to her parents, whom she'd not seen in several weeks. This was hardly the time to be thinking about the young rancher with sky-blue eyes. In fact, no time was a good time to let her mind dwell on the man, Maura told herself. But for the past three days, since she'd visited his ranch, daydreaming about Abe's grandson was all that she seemed to be doing.

After letting herself in, Maura passed through a long foyer and was entering a formal great room, when Regina, a tall, middle-aged woman with short, brown hair, appeared through an open doorway.

The woman spotted her immediately and gave her a little wave. "Well, look who's here! Are you lost or something?"

Chuckling, Maura hurried across the room to kiss the woman's cheek. For the past twenty years Regina had worked as a maid for the family. To the Donovans she was as much a part of the family as the six children were.

"I had a few chores to do in town," Maura explained. "So I thought I'd drive out and let everyone know I'm still alive. Are my parents home? And Grandmother?"

Reggie snagged a hold on Maura's shoulder and turned her toward the rear section of the house. "Fiona's here. But Doyle drove your grandmother to Ruidoso for a visit with the dentist."

"Oh, shoot," Maura practically wailed, then sighed with resignation. "I should have called beforehand."

Reggie said, "Well, the dentist visit was unexpected. Kate bit down on a piece of hard candy and chipped a tooth. Doyle practically twisted his mother's arm to make her go have it examined."

At age eighty-three, Kate Donovan was still in great health and just independent enough to think she didn't need anyone taking care of her. Maura had always admired her grandmother's spunk, especially after Arthur, her husband and Maura's grandfather, died eight years ago. Since then Kate hadn't waned or whined. She'd continued to have an input into the ranch her husband had founded more than forty years ago.

By now Maura and the maid had reached a point in the hallway where a wide opening led into a huge family room. With a flick of her hand, Reggie gestured toward the opening.

"Fiona is still in there, I think. Would you like me to bring in some fresh coffee, Maura? And I think Opal did some baking."

Maura smiled gratefully at the woman. "You're wonderful, Reggie. That would be great."

Moments later, as Maura stepped into the long room, she spotted her mother sitting at a small desk. Even from several feet away, Fiona's beauty radiated like a full bloomed rose. Her hair, threaded with silver, was still mostly black and wrapped in an elegant chignon at the back of her neck. A pair of dark slacks and pale pink blouse enhanced her slender figure.

Maura couldn't imagine looking so wonderful at fifty-nine years of age, especially after giving birth to six children and raising them to adulthood. But then Maura couldn't imagine herself with even one child. To have a family, she first needed a man. And after being so careful and turning down dates in her twenties, she'd done a miserable job when she'd chosen Gil.

Fiona must have heard her footsteps on the tile because she suddenly looked up from her work.

"Maura! Darling!"

The other woman put the ledger aside and rose to her feet. Maura hurried toward her mother's outstretched arms. After a brief hug, Fiona stepped back and gave her daughter a thorough glance. "My gracious! You look so rested and pretty! And that dress—I've never seen you wear anything like it."

For the first time in ages, Maura had felt a bit daring this morning. Instead of her usual jeans and blouse, she'd pulled a halter-styled sundress from her closet. The flowery fabric exposed Maura's back and arms and revealed a hint of cleavage. No doubt her mother was wondering about this new flirtatious image. Especially since Maura was considered the most reserved of the Donovan sisters and usually dressed the part.

"It's very warm out today," she said in a dismissive way, then took her mother by the hand and drew her down on a long couch upholstered in red suede.

"Your father and grandmother are at the dentist's office," Fiona explained. "They should be back well before dinner. Do you plan to stay?"

Having dinner with her big, boisterous family was probably just the thing Maura needed to get Quint Cantrell from her mind. But Abe would be looking for her to return soon and though he didn't demand her company every minute of the night and day, she wanted to get back to Apache Wells before a late hour.

"Not tonight, Mother. Abe will be expecting me."

Fiona grimaced. "You told me the man wasn't that ill. Surely you could be away for one evening," she argued. "Aren't there other people on the ranch who could watch out for him?"

Maura bit back a sigh. She wasn't in the mood to defend her job to her mother. She didn't want to have to explain to Fiona that her fondness for Abe was only part of the reason she'd chosen to live and work on Apache Wells. The problems she'd endured at the hospital with Dr. Weston were something she'd only shared with her sister Bridget. And she'd only discussed the matter with her because Bridget was a doctor and understood the nuances of medical life.

Before Maura had taken the job with Abe, Bridget had advised her to tell Dr. Weston to take his tacky flirting and go jump in the lake. And Maura had attempted to do that. Only in a nicer way. He'd not gotten the message and as

Maura had contemplated Abe's offer, she'd decided that even if Dr. Weston had gotten the message and quit pursuing her, the awkwardness of being around him would remain.

*Face it, Maura, you jumped at Abe's offer because you're afraid to deal with men. Because you're too much of a chicken to think about the dating game or confronting a man that might want you in a romantic way. You knew that you could hide on Apache Wells. Hide from men and your own failure as a woman.*

The mocking voice inside her caused Maura to instinctively stiffen her spine. Maybe taking the job with Abe had been an escape for her. But since then she'd developed deep feelings for Abe and he'd become an important part of her life. To Maura, that alone was enough to justify her job.

"Tonight isn't a good time, Mother. But I'll make a point to come out for supper soon. I promise."

Thankfully, Fiona didn't press the issue and after Reggie arrived with coffee and homemade pralines, their conversation turned to Maura's siblings and other happenings within the Donovan family.

A little more than an hour later, Maura bade her mother goodbye and was walking through the foyer to leave the house when her younger sister suddenly popped through the door.

"Maura!"

"Bridget!"

Both women laughed as their names came out in unison.

"Okay, you first, big sister," Bridget said. "What are you doing here?"

Maura gave her younger sister a brief hug. "I could ask the same of you. Aren't you working today?"

Bridget, who was somewhat shorter than Maura and had flaming copper hair, grinned in naughty fashion. "S-s-shh. I'm supposed to be back at the clinic by now. But I made a house call not far from here and I thought I'd stop by for a few minutes and see what I can swipe from the kitchen."

"Opal just made pralines," Maura told her.

"Sugar. That's not what I need," she said while patting a hand on her waist, then her green eyes sparkled as she took a closer look at Maura.

"My, my. You're looking sexy today. What's the occasion? Trying to give old Mr. Cantrell a heart attack or something?"

"Bridget! You're awful! You shouldn't be allowed to practice medicine!" Maura scolded.

Bridget laughed and Maura wondered how it would feel to be able to really laugh, to look at life with the same fun and excitement she'd once had. Perhaps if she'd been smart enough to avoid men entirely, the way her little sister had, she'd still be a happy woman.

"I've had a few patients tell me that very thing," she confessed with another chuckle.

Maura started to scold her again, but the cell phone in her purse suddenly rang. Quickly, she fished out the small instrument and was faintly surprised to see the caller was Abe.

"Excuse me for a moment, Bridget. I'd better take this."

Bridget lingered in the foyer while Maura exchanged a few brief words with the man. Once she'd ended the call, Bridget looked at her with concern.

"What's the matter? Who was that? You've gone pale."

As her sister shot questions at her, Maura slowly put the phone back in her handbag.

"It was Abe. He wanted to let me know that we're going to have company tonight."

"Is that all? From the look on your face I thought a tornado was about to hit. Who is this company anyway? Someone interesting?"

Maura did her best to wipe all expression from her face. "You might think so. It's Quint Cantrell. Abe's grandson."

"Mmm. I saw him not too long ago in Ruidoso," Bridget said thoughtfully. "I was pulling into a parking space on the street and he was coming out of the Blue Mesa. I have to admit he looks sexier now than he did when we were in high school."

Like a jolt of loud, unexpected thunder, jealousy shook Maura. "Then maybe you should join us for dinner," she quipped. "I'm sure you'd be more than welcome."

Unaware of her sister's reaction, Bridget playfully wrinkled her nose. "No thanks, sis. Quint obviously isn't into redheads with freckles. Actually," she added in a more serious tone, "I don't think he's into women. Period. Not after the wringer Holly put him through."

For the past few days that was exactly what Maura had been telling herself. The man didn't want a woman in his life. Yet during that short time she'd spent with him on the Golden Spur, he'd touched her, looked at her as though he'd actually wanted to be close to her. Or had that only been the twisted imaginings of a lonely divorcée?

One way or the other, Maura supposed she would find out tonight. And she wasn't ready for the answer.

"Maura? Are you all right?"

As Bridget touched her arm, Maura's thoughts jerked back to the present and she turned a strained look on her sister.

"Sure. Why wouldn't I be?"

Her gaze shrewdly studying Maura's face, Bridget shrugged. "I don't know. You tell me. Is something going on with Quint that you haven't told me about?"

Setting her jaw, Maura quickly turned and started toward the door. "Don't worry, little sister. If I see that Quint Cantrell is back into women you'll be the first to know."

## Chapter Four

An hour later, when Maura arrived back at Apache Wells, she was surprised to find Quint's pickup already parked next to Abe's old Ford. But once she entered the small ranch house, neither he nor Abe was anywhere to be found.

But before she could get to her room to change out of her revealing dress she heard voices on the porch, then footsteps entering the house.

"Maura! Where are you, girl?"

Abe's yells had her groaning as she turned from her room. Quint would just have to see her like this and she'd have to appear as though she was comfortable with exposing plenty of skin to his sharp gaze.

"Here I am," she announced as she stepped into the cozy living room.

Abe, who'd been reclining in his favorite leather chair, plopped his boots on the floor and let out a low whistle.

Across from him, sitting at one end of a long couch, Quint stared at her. Maura found it much easier to focus her gaze on the elder Cantrell.

"Ooooeee! Don't you look pretty!" The old man glanced over at Quint. "Look at her, boy. Have you ever seen anything so pretty around here?"

Quint's shocked stare couldn't decide if it wanted to settle on Maura or his grandfather. "Grandma wasn't exactly ugly," he reminded a grinning Abe.

Abe's grin turned into an impatient frown for his grandson. "Been many a long year since your grandma was with us. It's high time we had another pretty woman in the house."

Across the room, Maura cleared her throat and like a magnet Quint felt his gaze drawn to her slender image outlined by the open doorway. The flowered dress she was wearing made her look all woman and then some. His male ego wanted to think she'd worn the sexy garment for his benefit, but he knew otherwise.

"You should have warned me earlier that Quint would be here for supper," Maura said to Abe. "I would've gotten back sooner. It will take me a while to prepare something and—"

"Forget about cookin', honey!" Abe interrupted. "I didn't hire you as kitchen help! Jim has already fixed things. All we have to do is heat it up."

She looked surprised and Quint got the feeling that his grandfather probably manipulated his nurse as much as he tried to maneuver him. He could only wonder how long Maura would be willing to put up with the old man and what it would do to him when she flew the coop.

Maura said, "Oh. Well, I usually prepare our meals. You—"

"Tonight you're gettin' a rest," Abe interrupted again. "So don't worry about it."

A smile fluttered around her lips. "All right."

Abe motioned for Quint to get to his feet. "Go find us some of that blackberry wine and pour us all a drink, Quint. I feel like celebrating tonight."

Quint rose from the couch and ambled toward the doorway where Maura still stood. "What do you have to be celebrating?" he asked his grandfather.

"Bein' alive. Ain't that enough?"

Quint exchanged a pointed look with Maura and this time when she smiled the expression was genuine.

"I'll help you find some glasses," she told him.

He followed her down a short hallway and into the small kitchen. Along the way, he caught the rosy scent of her perfume as his eyes watched the folds of her dress move to the sway of her shapely hips.

Lord, it was no wonder Abe was behaving in such a goofy manner, Quint thought. Just looking at this woman was enough to send a man's temperature skyrocketing.

"I think the wine is over there," she said while pointing to a white metal cabinet situated at the far end of the room. "If you'll look for it, I'll find the wineglasses."

Drawing in a deep breath, Quint tore his eyes off her backside and headed to the cabinet. "Gramps hardly ever drinks spirits. I don't know what's come over him—he's acting strangely happy," he mumbled as he pushed aside cans and jars on the jammed pantry shelf. "Is it okay for him to drink this stuff, anyway?"

He pulled out the bottle of blackberry wine and walked over to the cabinet where she was placing goblets on a silver tray.

"A small amount won't hurt," she said, then slanted a

glance at him. "And why do you call Abe being happy strange? I'd think him being happy is a good thing."

It would be a good thing, Quint thought, if his grandfather's joy didn't depend on a woman. He'd learned through the years that they were fickle creatures and more often than not slanted the truth to their own advantage. Before their breakup, he'd caught Holly in several lies, yet she'd insisted she'd kept the truth from him because she'd loved him. He'd heard the same excuse from his own mother when he'd discovered she'd been dishonest about her past. Women never separated right and wrong with a clear line. They always wanted to soften and blur the edges with emotions and reasons. As though that would keep a man from feeling hurt and betrayed.

"I just don't want his bubble burst."

After twisting off the cap, he offered the wine bottle to her. She took it and carefully began to fill each glass with a small amount of the dark liquid. Quint's gaze fell to the shiny crown of her head and the dark red strands of hair lying on her bare shoulders.

"You think I'm going to do something to hurt your grandfather?" she asked.

He wasn't expecting such a direct question from her, but then he probably should have. She had a blunt way of getting things out in the open.

"Not necessarily. Sometimes Gramps just expects too much out of people. And when they fall short he gets disappointed."

She leveled her green gaze on him and Quint felt his heart pause, then jerk into a rapid thud.

"Have you ever disappointed anyone, Quint?"

What was the matter with him? Why did just watching

her speak feel like an erotic adventure? Sexual starvation, he thought. And that was a fixable problem.

"Hell, yeah," he answered. "Haven't you?"

Something flickered in the depths of her eyes before they dropped away from his.

"Oh, yes. More than I'd like to think."

She drew in a deep breath, then looked up at him one more time. "Whatever you're thinking, Quint, I'm here to help your grandfather. Not hurt him. As long as you understand that, I think you and I can be friends."

He wanted to be more than Maura's friend. When he'd come to that realization, he wasn't sure. Maybe just a few seconds ago when he'd looked at her moist lips. Or had it been minutes ago when he'd first looked up and saw her standing in the doorway, that dress hugging her breasts like the hands of a lover? Yes, he wanted to be more than Maura Donovan's friend and the idea was shaking the fire right out of him. She wasn't a casual sort of woman. But his body didn't seem to care one whit about that fact.

"I believe you're here to help Gramps. So let's not rehash the issue, okay?"

A slow smile spread across her face and Quint stifled a groan. If he could just kiss those luscious lips once, maybe twice, then he could hopefully put these crazy urges behind him.

"I'm perfectly agreeable to that," she said, then picked up the tray and offered it to him. "We'd better get back to Abe before he thinks we've deserted him."

Smiling to himself, Quint took the tray and followed her out of the room.

Much later, as the three of them finished coffee around the dinner table, Maura quietly listened while Quint and his grandfather discussed the pros and cons of allowing Red Bluff Mining Company to reopen the Golden Spur. Maura's knowledge about mining or taking gold from raw ore was practically nil, but from listening to their debate she could see that each man had good, solid reasons to back up his stand on the subject.

Throughout the meal, Maura had been a bit surprised to see that Quint wasn't a yes-man to Abe on any subject, even though the elder Cantrell was the patriarch of the family and held the strings to a fortune in land and money. Clearly Quint respected his grandfather, but he wasn't shy about speaking up when he didn't agree with the old man.

Maura admired Quint's spunk, but she was touched even more by the closeness and love she felt flowing between the two men. Gilbert had never shown much respect for his parents or tried to be a part of her family. She'd often voiced her disapproval about his lack of family connection and tried to make him see the joys he was missing, but her pleas had gone unheeded. One thing she knew for certain about Quint, he'd always be around for anyone he cared about.

"All right, Gramps, I'll call them. Maybe not in the next few days. But soon. And I'll get a rough estimate as to the initial cost to start things up. But that's all I'm going to promise. I'm not interested in gold," Quint was saying to Abe.

Maura smiled to herself as she saw Abe's eyes begin to twinkle. Clearly he believed he was the winner tonight.

"Maybe not. But the gold will make it easier for you to be a rancher. And it sure as heck might be nice to leave to your young'ns."

The muscles around Quint's mouth tightened, but he didn't make any sort of reply to his grandfather's suggestion. Maura wasn't surprised. When she'd brought up the idea of him raising children, he'd turned as cool as a frosty morning. Which could only mean he wasn't interested in acquiring a wife, much less kids.

Putting down his coffee cup, Abe stretched his arms over his head, then pushed back his chair. "Well, I'm gonna go watch a little news," he said. "Quint, why don't you take Maura down to the stables and show her the new stud. She's not seen him yet."

Fully expecting Quint to come up with an excuse to leave, Maura got to her feet and began gathering the dirty dishes. "That's all right, Abe," she said, not bothering to glance Quint's way. "I can walk down to the stables another time. It's almost dark anyway."

"It's at least another half hour until dark," Quint spoke up. "We have plenty of time."

Maura's gaze jerked to the end of the table just in time to see him rising from his seat. Instead of a look of boredom, she was surprised to see a smile on his face.

"Are you game?" he asked.

"Uh—sure." She glanced down at the plates she was holding. "Just let me put these away."

"I'll help you clear the table."

Flustered by this turn of events, Maura hardly noticed Abe quietly leaving the kitchen.

"There's no need," she told him. "I'll gather everything up later. We'd better not waste daylight."

She put the plates in the sink, then turned to see he was waiting for her by the door. As she joined him, her heart began to pitter-patter like a rain shower threatening to turn into an all-out storm.

"The evening might get cool before we get back," he suggested, his eyes sliding slowly over her bare shoulders. "Do you think you might need something to cover your arms?"

"You're probably right. Hold on," she told him, then hurried out of the room. By the time she fetched a shawl from her bedroom closet, she was breathless and silently berating herself for behaving like some besotted teenager. Quint Cantrell was merely being polite and friendly, she told herself. This was only a walk. Not a date.

Once the two of them were off the back porch and walking down the middle of the dirt road that led to the ranch yard, Maura breathed deeply and tried to relax.

"I really didn't expect you to go through with this," she said honestly. "I mean—Abe can be so obvious some-times. And he doesn't stop to think that you might have more important things to do than show me a horse."

Except for the crunch of gravel beneath their feet, the night was quiet. When Quint chuckled softly, the sound wrapped around her like the warm night air.

"I think showing you a horse is far more important than talking about that damned old mine. I was glad for an excuse to get away."

Smiling, she glanced at him. "Well, I understand you're not keen on inviting that sort of mining hubbub onto your ranch, but I think you're wonderful for listening to your grandfather's dreams and taking them seriously."

He shrugged as though he didn't warrant her compli-ment. "He's always listened to mine. And in spite of him being so cantankerous, he's a very wise man. I'd be a fool not to listen to him."

Too bad Gilbert had been so full of himself that he'd not looked to his family or anyone for advice, Maura thought. He'd believed himself to be smarter, slicker and savvier than anyone around him. And to a point, he had been, she thought grimly. He'd certainly fooled her for years. Was that what love did to a woman? Blinded her ability to see the truth, twisted her judgment? Until her love for him had begun to crumble, she'd not seen the real man.

"So how is your arm doing?" she asked after a moment. "I don't suppose you went to the doctor and got stitches."

"No. But it's healing."

It seemed the farther they walked, the closer he was drawing to her side. Maura tried not to notice, but that was fairly impossible to do when her heart was hammering in her chest.

"One of the best things I like about working for your grandfather is having time to be outdoors," she said. "Before, putting in long hours at the hospital didn't leave me much time or energy for walks outside."

"Did you do hospital work before you moved back to Hondo Valley?" he asked.

Before her divorce, she thought ruefully. Clearing her throat, she gazed ahead at a stand of tall pines and the long, dark shadows slipping across the road. Beyond the distant mountains, the sinking sun painted a bank of clouds pink and gold and as she admired the beauty, she realized she was just now coming awake after a long, long sleep.

"No. I worked at a large health clinic. Which was hectic, but rewarding."

"Forgive me if this sounds tacky, Maura, but we both know that you don't have to work at anything. I mean— your family has made millions and you're obviously wealthy. You could travel the world and be a lady of leisure."

She looked at him, then burst out laughing. "Oh, Quint. That's so funny. Me, a lady of leisure? I'd be bored out of my mind. And everyone has a reason for being, don't you think? I like to be doing—to make a difference for others. Don't you?"

He smiled and then his expression turned sober. "I guess I've never thought about it that much. I suppose from the time I was a boy I've been on a mission to keep the ranches going. As for making a difference for others—I must be selfish. I do what I do, because in the end, it pleases me."

Her eyes softened as she studied his face. "That's not entirely true, Quint. I don't know you all that well, but I can see that you want to make a difference for your grandfather, your mother. That's not a self-centered man."

One corner of his lips tilted to a wicked little grin. "You're wrong, Maura. I am selfish." One hand reached out and wrapped itself around her shoulder. "Because right now all I'm thinking about is what I want."

She shivered as heat rushed from the spot where he was touching her and shot to every particle of her body.

"And what is that?" she asked in a strained voice.

"To kiss you."

He watched her lips part with shock, but he didn't give her the chance to utter a word or move away. Placing a finger beneath her chin, he bent his head and settled his lips firmly over hers.

Soft. Incredibly soft. And oh, so sweet. Those thoughts tumbled through Quint's brain as his lips began to move against hers, to search for even more of her honeyed goodness. Mindlessly, his arms slipped around her waist and drew her ever closer.

Between them, he felt her hands flatten against his chest, then reach upward to his shoulders. The warmth of her spread through him like a white-hot sun baking his skin, heat seeping right down to his bones.

How long had it been since he'd kissed a woman? Since he'd wanted to kiss a woman? He couldn't remember.

Couldn't think. While his mind turned to mush, the rest of his body burst to life, buzzed as though her lips were liquid spirit, intoxicating, luring, begging him to surrender to the moment. To her.

Fired by a hunger that threatened to consume him, his hands pressed into her back and crushed her body up against his. Beneath his lips, hers opened like an exotic flower, tempting him to taste the center. When his tongue delved inside, she moaned low in her throat.

The feral sound matched the urgency inside him and it was all he could do to keep his hands anchored at her back instead of allowing them to cup her breasts, the swell of her bottom, to drag her hips forward and grind them against his aching arousal.

He wasn't sure how much time had ticked by when she finally pulled her mouth from beneath his and stepped back. For all he knew, it could have been long minutes or even hours since he'd first tugged her into his arms.

No matter, he thought, as he sucked in a harsh breath and tried to collect his senses. However long their kiss had lasted, it hadn't gone on long enough to suit him. Even though she was looking at him with stunned dismay, everything inside him was screeching for him to hang on to her, to capture her lips all over again.

*So much for kissing Maura and getting her out of your system, Quint.*

"I…think we'd better forget about walking on to the stables," she said in a breathless rush. Then before he could say anything, she turned on her heel and took off in long strides toward the house.

Before she could take three steps, Quint caught her by the shoulder and spun her back to him.

"Wait, Maura! We can't go back to the house now!"

Her breasts moved up and down as she struggled to regain her breath and Quint was amazed to find himself just as winded and shaken as she. As he watched her lips form a perfect O, he had to fight the urge to sear them back together with another kiss.

"We can't?" she murmured. "Why?"

"Because—" Heaving out another heavy breath, he shook his head. "After what just happened we—"

"Need to come to our senses and get back to safety," she finished for him.

His hands wrapped around her upper arms and held them tightly as though he wanted to make sure she couldn't escape.

"Safety? You think I… That we—our attraction is something to run from?"

She needed to run from herself more than him. But she couldn't admit such a thing. It would be like telling him she wasn't capable of controlling herself or her sexual urges whenever she was near him. Oh, God, how embarrassing.

"I think—" Twisting her head aside, she closed her eyes and tried not to think about the heavenly way he'd made her feel. So alive. So sexy. So wanted. "Things were about to get carried away, Quint. And I—I'm not ready for something like that."

There was a long pause, and while she waited for his reply, she tried to calm her racing heart, tried to tell herself that the kiss was no big deal. Even though it was the biggest thing she could ever remember happening to her.

"I never meant for the kiss to go so far, Maura," he said lowly. "That just seemed to happen."

Turning her face back to his, she opened her eyes and felt a jolt to her senses as she gazed into his blue ones. He was probably the most sexual, sensual man she'd ever met and to say that his kiss had been potent would be an understatement. Her knees were still quivering.

Mortified, she said, "I was in on it, too, Quint. It's just as much as my fault for letting it go on." And on and on, she mentally added.

"Why should it be anyone's fault? Why are you so bothered about this? It's not like we committed a crime—or hurt anyone."

She looked down at the ground while inside her emotions were tumbling, falling, rolling away at a speed too fast to allow her to catch up.

"That's true."

"And you did like it. As much as I liked it," he pointed out.

"I can't deny that," she admitted.

"So? Why are you trying to race back to the house? To end our walk?"

He called this a walk? She shivered to think what a deliberate rendezvous would be.

Her gaze dropped to the toes of his brown boots. "I shouldn't have to explain. But it looks as though I must." Her eyes fluttered back up to his. "I'm not the type to—well, just be a diversion for a man. And we both know that's all you want. A kiss, maybe two. Maybe you even want to have sex with me."

"The thought did occur to me."

Her nostrils flared at his flippant reply. "Well, it isn't going to happen."

Amusement dimpled his cheek long before a chuckle passed his lips. "That's what you think."

A mixture of annoyance and excitement rushed through her, pushing her heartbeat to an even higher rate. "And why? Why would you want a woman like me?"

Before he could answer, she twisted away from his grasp and began walking. By now it was growing dark and she could only think how easy it would be to fall into Quint's arms, to let him show her, remind her that she was still a woman. A woman who'd not been made love to in a long, long time.

He snaked an arm around her waist and once again forced her to stop in her tracks and face him.

"What does that mean? A woman like you?"

He brought his palms up to her face and Maura felt her knees threaten to buckle as he rubbed his thumbs against her cheeks. She was getting glimpses of what he would be like as a lover and those indications were far too tempting for a wounded woman like her.

"Oh, Quint," she said in a strained voice, "surely you can see what I'm talking about. For starters I'm six years older than you."

He frowned. "What does that have to do with anything?"

Maura rolled her eyes. "There's a gap between us."

"We can fix that," he drawled, then jerked her forward until the front of her body was brushing his. "See? No gap at all. In fact, I can tighten it even more."

He was being a hopeless flirt. Almost playful. Something she didn't think him capable of. Before this evening, the only Quint Cantrell she'd seen was a serious, work-driven man. She couldn't imagine what had brought about this change in him. Surely not her.

"There are other kinds of gaps, Quint. You're young and single." She didn't bother to add "rich, attractive and considered one of the biggest catches in Lincoln County."

"You are, too."

"I'm divorced," she said thickly.

"That doesn't make you contaminated."

She couldn't do anything but laugh and when a smile suddenly spread across his face, it made her feel good, better than she'd felt in a long, long while.

"See," he said, "you were taking one little kiss way too seriously."

The embrace that had gone on between them had been more than one little kiss. But he was right. The best thing she could do for both of them was to treat this whole thing in a casual way. The last thing he needed to know was that he'd shaken the very earth beneath her feet.

"You're right. I suppose I have been making too much of it."

The grin on his face deepened. "We still have a little twilight left. Let's walk on to the stables," he urged. "You don't want to have to tell Gramps you couldn't make it that far."

That wouldn't be nearly as embarrassing as returning to the house with red cheeks and swollen lips, she thought wryly. "All right. Let's go on. But—"

When she broke off with uncertainty, he quickly finished, "Don't worry, you've made it clear you've had enough kissing for tonight."

He slipped his arm across the back of her waist and as he urged her on toward the ranch yard, Maura could only think she might have Quint completely fooled, but not herself. She'd not had nearly enough of his kisses. Or his company. And with each step she took by his side, she wondered if she was headed toward a very special place or the hell of another heartache.

## Chapter Five

A few days later, as the weekend approached, Maura was considering driving over to the Diamond D on Saturday. Her mother was still hounding her about having supper with her family and Maura knew that Fiona wouldn't let up with her nagging until her eldest daughter showed up.

But on Friday evening Abe came in early from the ranch yard and spent the last waning hours of sunlight in his easy chair. The behavior was out of character and, though he insisted he felt fine, Maura suspected the man was dizzy but just didn't want to admit it to her.

Deciding she needed to stay close, Maura crossed the family meal off her plans and promised herself to go another time, when Abe wasn't behaving so peculiarly. But by Saturday afternoon, he appeared to be back to his normal self and raring to get back with the ranch hands.

Late that evening, sometime after dark, Abe was still out when she answered the phone and was vaguely surprised to hear Quint's voice. Since Abe carried his own cell phone, his relatives usually called him directly on it rather than over the landline.

"Hi," he said. "I was about to think you weren't in the house."

Just the sound of his voice caused her heart to trip over itself and she realized no man had ever made her feel so giddy and young.

"I was in the laundry room," she explained. "Abe is still down at the ranch yard. Did you try his cell?"

"I'm not calling to talk to Gramps," he answered. "I wanted to speak with you."

A warm flush swept up her torso and over her face. Since the night of their little kissing spree, she'd not seen or heard from him and she'd tried to write the whole thing off as a frivolous impulse on his part. There'd not been any other way to explain his behavior.

"Oh. Well, if you've been concerned about Abe, don't be. He appears to be back to normal."

"Concerned? I didn't realize anything had been amiss with Gramps. I talked to him this morning. He sounded fine. Has anything been wrong?"

"Not exactly. Yesterday he stayed indoors more than usual. That's all. But that appears to be over with now."

"Good. Then you wouldn't feel anxious about leaving the ranch for a few hours?"

Maura's mind raced ahead. What could he be getting at? "No. I wouldn't worry. Why?"

There was a long pause and then he spoke in a low voice that skittered lazily down Maura's backbone.

"Because I wanted to see if you'd like to come over to

the Golden Spur tomorrow. I've finally gotten a few of my good horses moved over here and I thought the two of us might take a ride. Maybe have a little picnic."

It was a good thing Maura had sat on the edge of the armchair when she'd picked up the phone, otherwise she would probably be collapsing with shock.

"You're inviting me on an outing?" she asked bluntly.

He chuckled. "Why not? I can't think of anybody else I'd rather ask."

What about asking no one and going on the ride alone, she silently asked. What about the guy who was so swamped with work he didn't socialize? The guy who wasn't that interested in women?

Her hands began to tremble ever so slightly and she gripped them tightly around each end of the telephone receiver in order to steady them.

"I don't know, Quint. It's been ages since I've been on a horse."

"More reason for you to accept my invitation. So you can get back in the saddle."

The heat in her cheeks grew hotter and she was very relieved he couldn't see her. "I thought you had lots of work to do," she countered. "That's what Abe is always telling me."

"He's right. My kind of work never gets caught up. But tomorrow is Sunday. After church, I don't work."

She'd not expected him to be a man who kept the Sabbath. But then she didn't really know everything there was to know about Abe's grandson. Other than he was as sexy as all get-out and the perfect picture of walking, talking danger.

Releasing a long breath, she passed the tip of her tongue over her lips. The other night, after they'd walked on to the horse stables, he'd remained a perfect gentleman. She couldn't believe the man was going to this much trouble just for a chance to kiss her again. Maybe he actually wanted her company? Liked her company? The idea thrilled her even more than the memory of their torrid kiss.

"Oh. Well, you make it sound like I shouldn't refuse."

"I'm not going to let you. Can you be here by twelve?"

If she went on this outing with Quint, what would Abe think? What would her own family think?

*You're a grown woman, Maura. This is nobody's business but yours. And it's high time you started acting like a woman instead of a fraidy cat.*

Bolstered by that idea, she blurted, "Sure. I can be there by noon. What do I need to bring?"

"Nothing, except yourself. Just be sure to wear heavy jeans and cowboy boots. Just in case you get too close to a jumping cactus."

She assured him that she'd be there at twelve and wearing appropriate riding gear, then they exchanged goodbyes. As Maura slipped the receiver back on its hook, she stared dazedly around the small kitchen, while a part of her wanted to dance and shout, laugh and run about the room like a wild thing that had just been let loose from a cage.

But she stopped herself short of expressing such exuberance. This wasn't the first date she'd been asked on since her divorce with Gilbert, she grimly reminded herself. One of the main reasons she was here on Apache Wells was because Dr. Weston had made a daily habit of asking her to go out with him. So why had she continually turned him down and jumped at the first chance she'd gotten to be with Quint?

Because when Dr. Weston had looked at her, talked to her, the only thing Maura had felt was annoyance. There'd been no sudden pounding of her heart or normally even breaths dissolving into soft little gasps. No heat firing her blood, urging her to touch, to move closer and even closer still.

Had she gone crazy? She'd run from Dr. Weston as though he was the devil incarnate and straight to Quint Cantrell. A man that made the good doctor seem as hazardous as downing a bowl of vanilla pudding.

The next morning, Quint slapped pieces of meat between slices of white bread sopped with mayonnaise, then covered them in plastic wrap and shoved them in a worn saddlebag. For dessert, he smeared peanut butter and jelly on wheat bread, wrapped the lot up and added them to the meat sandwiches. In the opposite saddlebag, he packed cans of beer and soda, then felt enormously proud of himself for remembering to add napkins.

He supposed he should have driven into town and purchased something special for the picnic meal. Like fried chicken and chocolate cake. But he was miles from town. And anyway, he didn't want to buy Maura's friendship. He wanted her to like him just for himself. Not because he was rich. Or young. Or good-looking. The last of which he'd never thought of himself, until she'd said such a thing to him the other night.

*The other night.*

Even now, days later, he could easily recall the way she'd felt wrapped in his arms, the way her lips had tasted against his. For a moment he closed his eyes as images and sensations assaulted his senses, filled him with hunger.

Maybe spending more time with Maura was asking for trouble. For the past four days, he'd been asking himself what he was doing by allowing himself to get so caught up in the woman. He'd not set out to get this involved. He'd only meant to kiss her, to prove to himself that she wasn't some sort of walking goddess.

But that kiss had done something to him and by the time it had ended he'd felt as though he'd been spun around in a violent whirlwind, then dropped into another world. Everything around him had suddenly seemed different, felt different.

Later, he'd realized he had to find out why she'd affected him so. Why one little red-haired nurse had put a spark in him like no woman he'd ever met.

With the saddlebags packed, Quint carried them down to the barn, where he began saddling two of his most dependable horses. He was tightening the back cinch on the last mount when a male voice sounded behind him.

"Hey, what's with the horses? You're not going to ride fence today, are you?"

Groaning inwardly, Quint turned around to see Jake standing a few feet behind him. He wished the other man hadn't shown up right now. Maura would be here soon and he'd just as soon not discuss his personal life with his old friend.

"No. I have something else planned," he told the other man.

"Oh. Well, I came by to see if you'd like to drive over to Bonito Lake and do a little trout fishing."

Resting his arm on the mare's rump, Quint stared at the other man. "Fishing? Since when have you taken up a rod?"

Shrugging, Jake turned his gaze toward the open doorway of the barn. "I used to like it. When I was young and Dad was still around."

"You've never told me that."

"No."

"So what made you want to go fishing today?" Quint persisted.

"Mom has been wanting some fresh trout. And she hasn't been feeling well." With a self-deprecating grin, he glanced at Quint. "I don't always just think of myself."

Quint figured most people thought of Jake as a rounder, a guy who was only out to have fun, but he knew there was another side to his old friend, one that he kept fairly hidden.

Quint smoothed his hand over the mare's rump. "Well, I would have liked to go with you," he said. "But I'm going on a picnic."

Jake chuckled. "Picnic, hell."

"Okay, let me rephrase this so you'll understand. I'm going riding and taking food with me."

"Man, you'd better get that redheaded nurse back over here to check your temperature. 'Cause you're definitely sick."

Turning back to the mare's side, Quint began to unnecessarily adjust the latigo. "You don't need to worry about my health, Jake. The redheaded nurse is going with me."

Quint could hear the other man's footsteps drawing closer.

"Maura Donovan? You're going riding with her?"

"That's right."

There was a very long pause and then Jake said, "A man only takes a woman he *really* likes riding."

Quint supposed Jake was right. The few women he'd tried to get interested in since Holly, he'd taken on traditional dates like dinner and a movie. During those outings, he been bored and wondering why he'd bothered in the first place.

"If you're asking if I like Maura, I do."

"Hmm. You gettin' serious about her?"

Faint unease stabbed Quint as he combed his fingers through the mare's black mane. "Me? Get serious about a woman? You know me better than that, ol' buddy."

"Yeah. How could I forget that you're a warped man? You don't have a decent thing to offer a woman."

Turning from the horse, Quint glared at the other man. "Don't you think you'd better head on to the lake? You can't catch a fish in the middle of the day."

Jake chuckled. "Aren't you lucky that term doesn't apply to a woman?"

Before Quint could make a retort, the other man turned and headed toward the open doorway.

"See you in the morning," he called out.

As Jake disappeared from view, Quint wondered if catching Maura was what he really wanted. If he did catch her, what would he do, besides the obvious? He didn't want a wife. At least, he didn't think he did. To be a good husband, a man had to invest a hell of a lot of himself.

At one time, when he'd been engaged to Holly, he'd thought that way of life was the way he wanted to go. His father, Lewis, had been a great husband and father. He'd been a happy man and he'd loved his wife until the last second of his life. Quint had wanted to follow his example. He'd wanted that same deep connection with a woman that his father had shared with his mother. But Quint had failed at a real love. Why the heck would he want to risk going through all that pain and humiliation over again?

*Because your house is empty. Your bed is empty. Your heart is empty.*

"Quint? Are you in here?"

Maura's voice jerked him back to the present and he

looked around to see she'd entered the cavernous barn. The sight of her was like a sudden ray of sunshine and at that moment he decided that today he wasn't going to analyze or fret over his motives toward Maura. A man didn't have to have a good reason to simply enjoy himself.

"Over here," he called to her.

Spotting him, she walked to the middle of the wide alleyway and stood while he led the horses over to her.

As he drew near, she asked, "Have you been waiting on me?"

The smile on her face was bright and lovely and made Quint feel so unexpectedly happy that he could have waited on her for hours and not complained.

"Not really. I've just now finished saddling the horses. And Jake came by for a few minutes."

"As I was driving in, I met a truck on the road," she commented. "I thought you might have had company this morning."

He grinned. "Jake isn't company. He's family."

"Yes. We Donovans have family like that, too," she said, then peered around his shoulder at the two horses. "Beautiful horses. Which one is mine?"

"The roan mare, Pearl. She's very smart and very mannerly. So I think you'll like her."

"I'm sure I will."

As she'd promised, she was dressed ruggedly in boots and blue jeans and a white shirt with the sleeves rolled back against her forearms. Her long hair was tied back from her face with a pale pink scarf and earrings made from polished cedar beads hung from her earlobes. Short of his mother, she was the only woman he knew that looked strong, yet utterly feminine at the same time, and in spite of himself he was totally drawn to her.

Using his head, he motioned toward the open doorway. "Shall we go? Do you have everything you'll need with you?"

"I brought saddlebags packed with a few things. They're just outside the barn door," she told him.

Once they were outside, Quint tied Maura's saddlebags onto the back of Pearl's saddle.

"I thought we'd ride over to Chillicothe. That's about five miles from here. Think you can go that far before we eat?"

She chuckled. "Shouldn't you be asking if I can make it that far? Period?"

He turned to face her and Maura was completely taken with the easy smile on his face, the fetching dimple in his cheek.

"Sorry. I wasn't thinking that you might not be hardened to riding. Can you make it that far?" he asked.

"I think so. If not, just tie me to the saddle and swat Pearl on the rump. The two of us will end up somewhere," she joked.

"I wouldn't think of putting Pearl through that sort of torture," he teased back, then added in a serious tone, "Don't worry. We'll take a break or two before we get there."

He handed her the mare's reins and she took a few moments to let the horse get accustomed to her smell.

"So where or what is Chillicothe?"

"A ghost town. It was built back in the mid-eighteen hundreds, when the Golden Spur was thriving. The old mine is just a short distance away from the town. I thought you might enjoy looking it all over."

"I'm sure I'll love it."

She led Pearl up a few steps, then lifted the reins over

her head. As she put her foot in the stirrup, she felt Quint's hands wrap around the sides of her waist. She wasn't expecting him to help her into the saddle and she glanced around with surprise.

"Pearl isn't that tall. I can manage," she assured him.

"My father always helped a lady into the saddle. So just in case he's watching I don't want to disappoint him."

With her toe still in the stirrup and her weight balanced on one boot, she paused long enough to allow her gaze to slide warmly over his face. "I'm very glad you invited me out today, Quint," she said softly.

"I'm very glad you're here," he replied, his gaze locking onto hers.

Feeling suddenly quite breathless, she cleared her throat and turned back to the horse. Taking her cue, he helped her into the saddle. Once he was confident that she was in control, he moved away and mounted his horse, a big brown gelding with a stripe down his nose.

"Chillicothe is to the northwest. This way," he said, motioning slightly to their left. "Not far from here, we'll hit the old road that led to the town. It's just a dim path now, but it makes for easy riding."

"Sounds great."

As they moved away from the barn, Maura swung Pearl alongside the big brown and the horses set out in an easy trot toward a pasture full of jumping choya. It was the time of summer for the plants to be in full bloom and the pink and yellow blossoms made for a pretty sight as they maneuvered their way through the prickly cacti.

"All of this area needs to be cleared away for pasture," Quint told her. "That's one of the things I'll be doing now that most of the barn and outbuildings are nearly finished."

"Oh, what a shame. The flowers are so beautiful."

"Yes, but there would be triple the amount of grass without them."

Maura cast him an impish look. "You're a practical man, aren't you? And not very much like Abe."

"Oh, I can loosen up—when I need to," he added.

She laughed. "Well, if you put a third less cattle on this particular range, then you could keep the flowers," she suggested.

Normally, Quint would have been quick to shoot down such a suggestion, calling it ridiculous and wasteful. But something about the pleasure she was gleaning from the cactus roses made him happy, made him reconsider even the smallest things around him.

"I'll think about that," he said.

Halfway through the ride to Chillicothe, they stopped near a deep arroyo. A shallow amount of water covered the rocky bottom while desert willows and twisted juniper grew at precarious angles from its loamy banks.

They rode down into the mini canyon, then dismounted and led the horses to the water's edge. The day had grown exceptionally warm and while the horses drank deeply, Quint shared his canteen with Maura.

Once the animals had their fill of water, they led them over to the bank and tethered the reins loosely around a willow limb.

After they were certain the horses were secured, Quint said, "I see a nice flat rock over there. Let's sit a few minutes before we head on to Chillicothe."

"Sounds good to me," she agreed. "Right now my legs feel like two pieces of rubber."

He offered his arm to her. "Here. You'd better hang on to me. Just in case you stumble."

"Thanks." She wrapped a hand around his forearm, then

quickly moved her clutch higher toward his elbow. "This is your cut arm," she explained. "I don't want to injure it again."

She could have torn the cut wide open again and Quint probably wouldn't have noticed. Just having her touching him again, walking close by his side, her body brushing against his was enough to send his libido into overdrive.

"Was my grandfather okay with you being gone from Apache Wells today?" Quint asked as he helped her get seated on the big boulder.

Smiling contentedly, she stretched her legs out in front of her. "He was more than okay. He was very happy."

He eased down beside her on the rock. "Hmmph. That's not surprising," he admitted. "Abe thinks I should show more interest in women. And he gets very disgusted with me when I don't."

Sighing, she looked up toward the sky. What had started out as nothing but bright blue sky this morning was now filled with fluffy white clouds.

"I know the feeling. Since my divorce, my mother thinks I should be out searching daily for another man." She shook her head. "She's been married to my father for nearly forty years. She has no idea how scary it would be without him."

Quint cast a curious glance her way. "Is it scary for you to be without your ex-husband?"

Her brows arched with faint surprise, she looked at him. "No. I know how to take care of myself. I just meant that it's scary to think about dating again. I guess—after Gilbert I don't trust men," she said, then swiftly shook her head. "That didn't exactly come out the way it should have. What I was trying to say is that I don't trust myself to pick the right man."

Oh, Lord, there had been so many times he'd felt that very same way, he thought. Choosing Holly had been one of the worst mistakes he'd ever made. And though Holly had done the cheating and the leaving, he still considered the whole affair as his mistake.

It had taken Quint quite a while to finally understand and admit to himself that he'd been blind and young where Holly had been concerned. He'd not been mature or wise enough to see that she'd been wrong for him in the first place.

Picking up a few pieces of gravel, he began to toss the tiny pebbles toward the pool of water. "You probably wouldn't want to tell me what happened to your marriage, would you?"

Even though he could only see her profile, it was enough to tell him that her expression had become shuttered.

"I wouldn't mind," she said, then glancing at him, her lips twisted sourly. "Gilbert married me for my money. I didn't know that at first. In fact, I didn't know it with certainty until the very end of our marriage. You see, he was a great actor."

"What do you mean by that?"

"Maybe I should start from the first to explain," she told him. "I'd been working at a clinic in Alamogordo when I first met Gil. We dated for about four months before I finally decided to accept his marriage proposal. Which was impulsive for me. Up until I met Gil I was very cautious about my relationships with men. But he'd come along at a time when I wanted to get on with my life and he'd been so attentive, so considerate of my needs and wants. He kept reassuring me that he wasn't interested in my money and I foolishly believed him. After all, he earned a good salary of his own and he never asked me for anything that was connected to finances."

"You're a rich woman, Maura. You never had suspicions about his motives?" His brows pulled together. "Damn, you must have been a trusting soul."

She groaned with regret. "That's what I meant about being a good actor. Gil was the sort that could make a person believe the sun was shining in the middle of a rainstorm. Even Mother believed he was sincere. But Daddy totally disapproved of him. He described Gil as slicker than an oil pit. At that time I thought Daddy was just being overly protective with his daughter. But unfortunately, it turned out that Daddy was right and I was the naive one. I believed Gil truly loved me."

He caught the sound of self-deprecation in her voice and was amazed at how much that sound depicted his own feelings.

"So how did you learn he'd married you for your money? Weren't there signs on the wall that you could have read?"

Maura answered ruefully, "There was nothing about Gil that appeared out of line. Until after we were married. And even then I didn't think it suspicious when he wanted to use our money—or technically you could call it my money—to buy luxury items like vehicles and boats and exotic vacations. He always reasoned the purchases away by insisting he wanted me to have the best of things. Because he loved me. Because I worked so hard as a nurse that I deserved them." Full of shame, she looked at him. "I couldn't see through him, Quint. I wanted to believe that he loved me so much he merely wanted to spoil me with gifts. I didn't want to consider, even for a moment, that he was in the marriage for ulterior reasons. But as time went on I couldn't ignore his lavish spending. Then finally I started asking myself if he was really buying these things for himself and using me as an excuse."

"How did you discover the truth?" he asked gently.

She let out a long sigh. "It all happened over the course of two or three years," she told him. "But the turning point began when I wanted to get pregnant and have a child."

Struck by that, he turned toward her. "He didn't want children?"

Shaking her head, she said, "Gil's job had him traveling at least three or four days out of the week, sometimes more. We both agreed that wasn't conducive to raising a family. So I promised to wait and he promised to put in for a desk job that would allow him to stay home. But year after year began to pass and everything stayed the same. He always came up with excuses as to why he couldn't change jobs within the company."

His expression stern, he said, "Maybe he resented the fact that you were working at a career you liked while you expected him to change jobs? What did he think about you working?"

"He did resent me asking him to change—but I didn't find out about that until—" She paused, then went on bitterly, "Well, until later. But as for me working, he was all for it. My job kept me occupied and out of his way. So that he'd be free to do his own thing."

"I think I see," he said thoughtfully. "So what did you do?"

She turned her palm upward in a helpless gesture. "I began to question him and he promptly accused me of nagging." Bending her head, she said in a strained voice, "Most women want to bear a child, Quint. That's all I wanted. But he couldn't even give me that much."

The pain in her voice stabbed him right in the middle of his chest. What kind of man would want to hurt this woman, lose this woman? he wondered.

"That's why you divorced him?"

She grimaced. "That was only a part of it, Quint. I found out…at the clinic where I worked, I accidentally overheard a couple of nurses discussing us. They were saying how sorry they felt for me because he'd had so many women during his travels and I didn't seem to know."

"What they were saying could have been unfounded gossip," he reasoned.

"That's what I wanted to think. But I confronted Gilbert about it and he confessed. He'd never intended to take a desk job or have a family. He liked things as they were. In short, he wanted his fun and a rich wife on the side."

"Sounds like a real nice bastard."

Her expression was stark as she turned her head and looked at him. "See. A man like that—I should have known all along. From the very first my father tried to warn me about Gilbert. But I was so blinded I wouldn't listen to him. I let love lead me around by the nose. And now—well, I'm not going to let that happen again."

Her firm vow sounded like so many he'd made to himself. And yet he had the strangest urge to tell her she shouldn't be bitter or wary. She was a gentle and lovely woman and some man would eventually come along and love her. Really love her. So why wasn't he thinking that about himself? he wondered wryly. He was a good and honest man. Why didn't he believe a good, sincere woman would come along and love him?

Quint couldn't answer that question. He didn't even try. Instead, all he could say was, "I understand where you're coming from, Maura."

Twisting her body toward his, she reached over and clasped his hand between hers. The unexpected touch warmed him, excited him in ways he'd couldn't explain.

"Do you, Quint? You and Holly—"

"Weren't compatible," he finished for her. "Mainly she wanted a different lifestyle than me. A rancher's day-to-day grind wasn't glamorous enough for her."

Maura frowned. "Everyone around here knew you would always be a rancher. Surely she didn't think you would change that for her."

Grimacing, he shook his head. "No. We'd been dating since high school, but when we got engaged we were both in our senior year of college and I was earning a degree in agriculture business. She had hopes that I would put that to use in other ways than a hands-on rancher. She saw me becoming an executive for some cattle-buying firm or working my up to a prestigious position in the equine business. Or even just sitting back and managing the ranch from an office."

A faint smile curved her lips. "I can't see you doing any of that. You're an outdoor man."

He grunted cynically. "Holly never understood that about me. She also believed we'd make our home at the Chaparral. I explained that I considered that my parents' home and I wanted something of my own. And when I made it clear that I wanted something far more modest than the Chaparral, she didn't hide her disappointment in me. In her opinion, I gave her plenty of reasons to look elsewhere. And maybe I did. But a man can't compromise his basic roots."

"Well, if I remember right the Johnsons were well-off," Maura reasoned. "I guess Holly's parents had always given her whatever she wanted. That's never a good thing."

Quint grimaced. "I thought her family being well-off meant that she couldn't be interested in my money. Not when she already had her own. I was a fool for not realizing that people like Holly always want more. I suppose when she met that rich real estate guy up in Denver she saw her chance to get everything she wanted. It didn't matter that he was nearly twice her age." Sarcasm twisted his features. "She would consider my little house on the Golden Spur a shack. But you know what, it's me and I like it. I wouldn't change it for her. For anyone."

"You shouldn't have to," she said softly.

Her fingers moved gently over the top of his hand as though she wanted to console him in some way. But Quint could have told her that he didn't need that sort of comforting from her. He wanted her lips fastened to his, her body crushed beneath him. The thought of making love to this woman was beginning to consume him and make everything else seem very unimportant. That couldn't be healthy. But he'd already gone past the point of stopping it.

He sighed. "Since Holly, I've met a few women who thought they could change me. In a way, I guess I've had the same sort of problem that you had with your ex. Most of the women I've dated seemed to equate Cantrell money with easy living. But that's not what I'm about, Maura."

"No," she said gently. "I can see you're not that sort of man."

He believed her and that in itself was scary. He wasn't expecting this woman to be able to read him, empathize with him. He'd looked for her to be cut from the same cloth as the rest that had come and gone in his life. The fact that she was so different knocked him totally off guard.

Clearing his throat, he tugged on her hand. "Well, time is getting on, we'd better mount up," he told her.

With his hand beneath her elbow, he helped her across the rocky ground and over to where the horses stood tethered in the shade. After a few minutes of untying reins and tightening girths, they were ready to mount up and Quint automatically moved behind Maura to assist her into the saddle.

He was about to reach for a hold on her waist when she suddenly turned to face him. And as he found his face close to hers, he felt his heart thudding hard and fast. She was looking at him with eyes as soft as a summer night.

"I just wanted to thank you, Quint. For listening to my troubles. I used to be terribly embarrassed for anyone to know that Gilbert chased after other women." Her long lashes fluttered demurely downward to hide her green eyes. "For a long time I thought—well, that I must be lacking as a woman. Now I'm beginning to believe that he was the one who was lacking something. Not me."

Quint couldn't stop himself from groaning as his hands settled on her shoulders. "Oh, Maura, you're lovely and sexy and I want to kiss you. Very much."

Maura didn't stop to think or even speak. She simply closed her eyes and leaned into him. And when his lips came hungrily down on hers, something inside her melted like a sand castle beneath a wash of tide. He swept her away, made her forget, made her long for all the things she'd been trying to forget.

Expecting the kiss to turn as torrid as it had the other night when he'd visited Apache Wells, Maura was surprised when he soon lifted his head and gave her a crooked grin.

"We'd better mount up this time," he said huskily. "Before I forget where we are."

Unable to do much more than nod, Maura turned to Pearl and, with Quint's help, climbed into the saddle. But as the two of them rode out of the quiet arroyo, all she could think about was being in his arms.

## Chapter Six

Chillicothe consisted of five buildings grouped together in one small area and split by a dimly rutted road that, back in the town's heyday, had probably been considered the main street. These days, tall sage and prickly pear had taken over most of the roadway.

As Quint and Maura rode through the ghostly village, she looked around with keen interest.

"This is very neat—having an old mining settlement on your property," she said.

He shrugged. "It can also be a nuisance. Gramps and I are often approached about opening the place up to tourists. Some even suggest rebuilding it into a wild west town and charging admission. Can you imagine what a circus that would cause around here?"

"I wouldn't like it," she admitted. "What does Abe think?"

"Thank God he agrees with me on that issue. This little town is just like a grave site. It shouldn't be trampled on by a bunch of strangers."

Shaded by several tall cottonwood trees, the largest building of the lot had once been a company store and directly across from it, the swinging doors of an old saloon had long ago fallen from their hinges and landed on the planked porch. Down the street three more buildings were partially standing, one of which appeared to have been a blacksmith shop. Part of a forge was visible in the open doorway.

"We'll come back in a few minutes for a closer look and have lunch," he told her. "Right now let's ride on to the mine. It's just a short distance from here."

"Fine," she agreed.

After leaving the remnants of Chillicothe, they rode northwest for another quarter of a mile. Here the landscape changed to low mountains covered with short grass, a sprinkling of orange and purple wildflowers and a few pines.

When they reached a small creek trickling with crystal clear water, Quint said, "Back in the eighteen hundreds the miners first found gold panning this little creek. But it was a long time afterward before they began to dig for it."

Bemused, Maura looked down at the stream. "I wonder if any nuggets are still around?"

"You're welcome to pan," he teased.

Laughing, she looked over at him. "No thanks. I might get the fever and then I'd have to set up camp out here."

The grin slowly faded from his face. "That might not be a bad thing. Then I wouldn't have to make excuses to see you."

Since their stop at the arroyo, something had changed

between them, Maura thought. She didn't know exactly what it was or what had brought it about. But with every beat of her heart she could feel herself drawing closer and closer to this man. With every breath she took, the protective wall she'd built around her was crumbling away into useless rubble.

"You mean showing me Chillicothe and the mine was just an excuse to see me?" she asked.

His low chuckle was both sensual and suggestive and Maura's cheeks burned with self-conscious heat. In her younger days, she'd never had trouble attracting the opposite sex and even since her divorce from Gilbert, she'd been asked on dates by a few men. But she could safely say none of them had been half as masculine or sexy as Quint. And just the idea that a man like this young rancher wanted her company rattled her senses.

"No. I honestly wanted you to see them," he admitted with a grin. "Having your company is a nice addition." He motioned for her to follow him across the creek. "Come on. The mine is just around this next hill."

Maura was surprised when the entrance to the Golden Spur finally came into view. From all the talk that Abe had been doing about the mine, she'd expected something far more grand than a small hole in the side of the mountain.

Like the buildings in the nearby ghost town, the lumber used to frame the entrance had now weathered to little more than gray pieces of wood. In some places the nails had rusted completely away and the boards looked as though a strong puff of wind would cause them to collapse. But above the dark entrance, a large piece of tin with the name of the mine was still erect and dark enough to read.

After they dismounted and tethered their horses on an old broken wheel that someone had discarded, they walked near enough to the entrance to peer inside.

"So this is what has Abe all stirred up," Maura said with amazement. "It doesn't look like much from here."

"It probably isn't. As far as I know no one has been inside to do any type of work since back in the 1950s. At that time the miners weren't pulling enough gold out to warrant keeping the thing open. But for some reason Gramps believes there are more veins of gold ore to be found here. Why, I don't know," Quint said wryly. "He just gets these hunches."

"Well, from what he's told me about his oil-drilling days, he's had some good hunches." Bracing her hand against one of the sturdier boards, Maura stuck her head inside and tried to peer into the dark cavern. "Can we go inside?"

"You mean you'd want to?" he asked with a bit of amazement.

"Sure. I'm not a scaredy cat." As long as losing her heart to a man wasn't involved, she thought. Though, she had to admit that the longer she hung around Quint, the more she was feeling the danger.

"Well, want to or not, it wouldn't be safe. A few months ago, I went a short distance inside and from what I could see the timbers appeared to still be intact, but I'm sure the years have compromised their sturdiness. Since no one knew I was out here, I decided it would be foolish to explore any deeper."

"Do you have any idea how far the mine goes back into the mountain? I'll bet you could probably find old maps through county archives."

"Gramps has a copy of one of the most recent maps

made. There's a network of shafts in there, but I don't remember how deep they go. A fair distance, I think."

She turned away from the dark cave to find Quint standing a few inches behind her and she wondered if he realized how tempting he was, how much she wanted to reach out and connect to him, even in the most simple ways.

Drawing in a breath, she asked, "Have you decided anything about bringing in the mining company to reopen the Golden Spur?"

His gaze narrowed keenly on her face. "I haven't. Not yet. Why?"

She smiled gently. "Just curious. And if you're thinking I'm going to take Abe's side of things, you're wrong. I'm not going to take yours or his. This old mine is between the two of you. The only thing I will say is that I can see pros and cons either way."

He chuckled. "Very diplomatic, Maura. Maybe you should have been a politician instead of a nurse."

She laughed along with him. "Well, my dad set me on a fence long before he put me on a horse. So I learned to straddle it first."

His hand wrapped around her shoulder and she felt her breath catch in her throat as his fingers gently kneaded her flesh.

"Thank you, Maura. It feels good to be able to laugh and not take the mine issue so seriously."

As she looked into his eyes, nerves fluttered in her stomach and unconsciously the tip of her tongue came out to moisten her lips. If he kissed her again, as he had in the arroyo, she didn't know if she could hide the desire that was subtly simmering deep within her. "It feels good to me to be here and forget about a lot of things."

Suddenly clearing his throat, he urged her away from

the cave door. "Let's go have our lunch. I don't know about you, but I'm starving."

Yes, she was starving all right, Maura thought. And she'd not realized just how much until Quint had stepped into her lonely life.

By the time they rode back to Chillicothe, the clouds overhead were pulling together to form a gray, menacing sky. After leaving their horses in the shelter of the old blacksmith shop, they carried their saddlebags down to the mercantile building.

Maura was totally surprised when Quint opened the door and she stepped inside to see an old table and chairs in the middle of the large wooden floor.

"I know this hasn't been here since the town was deserted," she declared.

"No. Jake and I hauled it out here. This building is in the best condition of all of them, so we chose it to fix up for a line shack. You never know when an electrical storm or a blizzard might blow up and it's good to have a place to shelter or even spend the night, if need be. We have candles, kerosene lanterns, firewood and some canned goods and bedding all stored in the back."

"This is neat," she said as she gazed around her at the rows of dusty shelves lining the walls and a long counter running across the back. "We can leave the door open for light and it will almost be like we're eating outside."

Quint slanted her a rueful glance. "Unfortunately we only have an outhouse for a bathroom. It's behind this building just in case you need it. But there's piped water from a nearby spring for washing. You'll find it at the side of the building near a wooden water trough."

"Thanks," she told him. "I'll be right back."

When she returned he had sandwiches laid out on the tabletop, along with four cans of beverages. In the middle of the table, a fat candle held by a shallow jar lid was now lit and the glow of the flame helped chase away the gloom of the threatening rain clouds. She'd been present at a few candlelight dinners before, but none had been quite like this. And Maura realized the quaintness of their surroundings had only a small part to play in the specialness of the meal. It was Quint who was making it all so unique. Quint who was making her very aware of their isolated setting.

He helped her into one of the chairs and as she thanked him, he said, "I'd better warn you that the food is sorta sloppy. I'm not too good with kitchen duties."

"I can eat most anything," she told him. "And I brought a few things, too. Potato chips, candy bars and brownies."

"That sort of bad stuff? From a nurse?" He chuckled as he took the chair across from her. "Where did you pick up such nasty habits?"

Laughing along with him, she said, "S-s-shh. Don't tell anyone, but we nurses don't always follow doctor's orders."

"I'm glad to hear that. Now I won't feel guilty about stuffing myself."

Quint passed the sandwiches and drinks between them and they began to eat.

After Maura had downed a few bites in silence, his expression turned rueful.

"What are you thinking?" he asked. "That the sandwiches are soggy?"

"I couldn't have made better," she assured him with a smile, then added thoughtfully, "I was just trying to picture the people who used to live in this little town. I wonder if there were whole families who made their home here? Babies born here?"

He shrugged as he reached for one of the beer cans. "Probably. I think there was a population of about three hundred at one time. There's another area just to the south of these buildings where you can find old foundations and other signs of houses. Gramps says not long after he purchased the land a fire swept through here, so the home sites might have burned. Thankfully that was many years after this little community died."

She sighed wistfully. "Well, when the place was booming it must have been an exciting time for people. Each morning they probably climbed out of bed thinking today they'd discover the mother lode."

He leveled a suggestive grin at her. "Why, Maura, you sound like a gamble excites you."

He excited her. And he was definitely a gamble, she thought as her heart danced rapidly against her ribs.

"Funny you should say that. I'm considered the cautious little mouse of my family." Her gaze fluttered awkwardly down to the planked tabletop. "And I suppose I am. I've never been one to play the odds—at anything. Out at the mine I told you I wasn't a scaredy cat, but that was sort of an exaggeration. I'd like to be more adventurous, but I guess I'm just a sure-thing sort of person."

"You got married," he said softly. "I'd say you were adventurous."

A cynical grimace tightened her lips. "Marriage isn't supposed to be a risk. At least, I thought it wasn't. I figured I knew all the important things there were to know about Gil. But I guess a person sometimes takes chances when she doesn't even realize she's doing it."

The corners of his mouth tilted into a faint smile.

"That might be a good thing. Otherwise, we'd all be living in bubbles."

Normally, Maura didn't eat mayonnaise, but as she took another bite of the sandwich that Quint had made, she was surprised at how much she liked the taste. She was even more surprised at how much she was beginning to like him. Which was something completely separate from being swept away by his kiss.

"What about you, Quint? Are you a man who takes chances?"

"Only when I need to."

His answer was evasive, but Maura didn't prod him. Today was the most special day she'd had in a long, long time. There was no need for serious talk. This was a day to simply enjoy.

"That was a silly question from me," she said after a moment. "Ranchers take risks every day. Dad always says that raising horses is like raising children—the job is hard as hell and you never know if any of them will turn out to be worth a damn." She let out a short laugh. "But he loves us all—the horses and the kids—no matter if we aren't stars."

He looked at her quizzically. "Surely you don't think you're any less important than your siblings?"

One of her shoulders lifted and fell. "Did I say that?"

"Not in so many words. But there was something in your voice." He reached across the table and touched his fingers to hers. "I sometimes get the feeling, Maura, that you're down on yourself."

The touch of his fingers was like a branding iron, sizzling a fire right through her hand and straight up her arm. He couldn't possibly know how shaky and vulnerable he made her feel.

"My sisters are special. They're both very beautiful

and spunky. They go at life at full speed. I'm…just drifting."

He frowned at her. "That's plain wrong. You have a meaningful, admirable profession. You're young and intelligent and very lovely. And you're not drifting—unless you consider seeing after Gramps trivial."

Surprise parted her lips. "Oh, no! I didn't mean that at all. Abe is very important to me. I just meant that personally I'm drifting." She sighed with a bit of frustration, then tried her best to smile. "I'm not down on myself, Quint. Just a little disappointed in the mistakes I've made."

Unable to bear the burning touch of his fingers any longer, she pulled her hand away and reached for a plastic bag filled with brownies.

"Aren't we all?" he murmured.

Her eyes locked with his and suddenly her heart lifted and a soft smile curved her lips.

"Yes," she said huskily, then deciding it was time to change the subject completely, joked, "Is there a coffee house down the street? Coffee would be great with all these desserts we have."

"We don't have to go down the street, my lady. We can make coffee right here." His eyes twinkled as he popped the last of a sandwich into his mouth and rose to his feet. "Come here. I'll show you."

She followed him to where the long counter separated the front of the room from the back. Behind the L-shaped barrier she was surprised to see a cast-iron potbellied stove and a small metal cabinet filled with canned food and basic staples for cooking. On the opposite side of the space, jammed in an out-of-the-way corner, an army cot covered with a faded Navajo blanket served as a bunk.

Clearly, Quint had taken special efforts to make the place comfortable for him and the hired hands.

With his money, he could have gone overboard and rebuilt the whole structure. He could have supplied it with electricity, a bathroom and all the comforts of home. Instead, he'd chosen to keep the old building simple and full of character. He didn't need or want everything he had to be new or perfect. And she realized she liked that very much about him.

"This is all very neat," she told him. "Have you ever stayed here overnight?"

He chuckled as he shoved a few sticks of wood into the stove. "Once. About a year ago when Jake and I first started building the ranch. The two of us got caught out here in a blizzard and we ended up sleeping on the floor in our bedrolls and freezing our behinds. After that, we decided to fix this place up."

He stuck a match to the kindling and when tiny flames began to lick at the sticks of wood, he shut the door on the stove and turned the damper wide.

"You're very close to Jake, aren't you?"

"He's like a brother to me," he said as he fetched a sack of coffee from the metal cabinet.

"Is that why you have him working for you?" she asked.

A faint grin touched his mouth as he filled the granite pot with water from his canteen. "I have him working for me because he knows everything there is to know about horses and cattle and can do more than three men put together. He was making good money at the track, working as manager over the training barns. But I was fortunate enough to talk him into helping me."

"Hmm. From what I can see, you two are so different. How did you get to be such good friends?"

He poured a hefty amount of grounds into the water, then set the pot on the stove.

"In kindergarten and grade school we constantly whipped up on each other. He was always lipping off, daring me to do something I shouldn't do. And I was the quiet one who exploded when he pushed too far. After a while, we both realized that neither could beat the other one up and we earned each other's respect." He looked at her and chuckled. "Thankfully, we don't test each other anymore. Now that we're grown men, I'm not sure who'd win. But I do know we'd fight *for* each other."

She gravitated toward him and the heat that was now radiating from the stove. "I wish I could say I had a friend like that. But I don't. In school, I guess you could say I was a loner of sorts. I had friends, but I didn't build deep bonds with them. I saved all that for my sisters. The three of us are very close."

"There's nothing wrong with that. My sister is my buddy, too. Although I don't get to see her much now that she's moved to Texas. Abe is trying to lure her and Jonas back, but I don't think he'll get that done. You see, Jonas is a Texas Ranger."

"Abe tells me that you've driven him to San Antonio a couple of times to visit them," Maura said. "If I remember right, he said the two of you made the trip to see Alexa and Jonas's new daughter shortly before he started suffering from vertigo. That's a long drive to make."

Quint shrugged. "Gramps won't fly. He says he doesn't want to get any higher off the ground than a horse's back. And when he dies he wants it to be with his boots on. But

I don't want to think of him dying in any fashion. I want to think of him living to be a hundred."

Maura smiled gently. "And he's just ornery enough to do it."

His gaze met hers. "Yeah. He is."

Something in his eyes, the softness in his voice, drew her to him in a way that was somehow even deeper and stronger than his kiss.

It was a strange sensation and so unsettling that she finally had to turn away and draw in a calming breath.

Behind her, she heard him move away, then the scrape of cans being pushed around the metal shelf. Glancing over her shoulder, she saw that he was putting away the sack of coffee grounds. Nearer to her, in the corner of her eye, she could see part of the makeshift bed and though she tried to keep her mind off it, she couldn't stop herself from imagining how it might feel to lie with him here in the quietness, to feel his hands and lips moving over her body.

"Oh, hell! It's going to storm!"

Quint's exclamation had her spinning around just in time to see a huge gust of wind ripping through the doorway and snuffing out the candle on the table. Except for the light coming from outside, the space around them suddenly went dim and shadowy.

"I'll get the door!" he shouted as he rushed around the counter and hurried to fasten the door.

Maura raced after him and peered through the slatted boards covering the empty squares that used to hold glass windows.

A wall of blue-black clouds was descending upon them at a rapid rate. Cold wind was tearing down the street, ripping clumps of dry sagebrush from the soil to send them rolling in erratic trails toward the opposite end of town.

"Oh, my, Quint, this looks like it's going to be nasty!"

She'd hardly gotten the words past her mouth when a streak of lightning bolted across the sky and sent her leaping backward from the rickety window. Deafening thunder followed and she wrapped her arms protectively around herself as she waited for the sound to subside.

With the door latched as securely as he could manage, Quint walked over to her. Her face was pale with alarm and he instinctively reached out and circled his arm around her shoulders.

"We'll be fine," he tried to reassure her. "And the horses are safely sheltered away from the lightning. So we don't need to worry about them."

She looked up at him and tried to smile, but he could see her lips were quivering with the effort.

"I'm okay, Quint. I'm not normally afraid of storms. But in this flimsy old building, the force of it just feels closer."

He gave her an encouraging grin. "Just think of it this way, Maura. This old store has been here for more than a century. Why should it crumble around us now?"

"Why indeed?" she asked, then just as she was trying to laugh at their predicament another clap of thunder rattled the roof far above their heads. "Oh!"

Grabbing her hand, he urged, "Let's go to the back. The building is studier there. And the coffee is boiling over. I've got to get the pot off the stove."

By the time they rounded the counter, rain was driving against the old walls with a shuddering force. Behind them, water began to pour through the cracks in the roof and pelt the food they'd left lying on the table.

"You stay here by the stove," he ordered after he'd dealt with the coffeepot. "I'll gather up our food from the table."

"No!" she cried, clutching his arm. "Please. Stay here with me. We don't need the food!"

Seeing she was becoming really frightened, he wrapped his arms around her and pulled her tightly against his chest. "All right, Maura," he said close to her ear so that she could hear him above the deafening sounds of the storm. "I'll stay right here. Close your eyes, honey. Imagine you're somewhere nice and sunny. Like on a beach. In a bikini. With me rubbing oil on your back."

After a moment her shoulders began to shake and when he eased his head back and looked into her face, he could see she was trying to laugh through her fear.

"That's a wicked thought, Quint Cantrell."

He kneaded her back while the heat of her body snuggled up against his was a damn sight hotter than the crackling fire in the stove. Even hotter than the lightning crackling around the old building.

"Hmm. A very nice one, too."

Her head tilted back from his chest and as he looked down into her eyes, he felt something sweet and hot and protective sweep through him all at the same time.

"I— The lightning, Quint. A bolt of it hit too close to me once when I was out riding with my brother Brady. I was knocked from my horse and wasn't breathing. If he hadn't known CPR—"

She broke off with a shudder and he didn't ask her to finish. He didn't have to. He understood her fear and admired her for not falling completely apart.

"I'm not going to let anything hurt you. I promise."

Her arms slid around his waist and clung tightly, her face buried into his shirt. The fact that she trusted him, that she was seeking him for comfort and security, swelled his chest and touched his heart in a way that it had never been touched.

"I know," she said, her voice muffled. "Just hold me."

Quint gladly obliged her request and after a few minutes, the lightning began to subside, even though the rain continued to pour. With the thunder drawing farther and farther away, he could feel Maura began to relax in his arms.

And then everything suddenly began to change. Her hands started to move against his back, her head tilted backward, her lips parted. Something deep and hot and primitive began to beat inside him, and with a needy groan he dropped his head and covered her mouth with his.

Quint didn't know if the storm had charged the air around them, or if the desire between them was setting off sparks. Either way, the fire inside him had already ignited and he wasn't about to try to extinguish it.

The kiss he gave her was long and hungry and by the time their mouths finally parted, they were both breathing heavily and staring at each other in shocked wonder.

Finally, Maura lifted her hand to cup the side of his face. "Oh, Quint," she murmured. "Being with you—like this—is…special. So special."

Feeling raw and naked and unexpectedly emotional, Quint thrust his fingers into her hair and against her scalp. Then holding her head motionless, he lowered his lips back to hers.

This time he gentled his searching mouth and took his lazy time drinking in her sweet taste, while an ebb and flow of desire rushed through him like a high tide threatening to drown everything in its path.

When he finally broke the kiss and lifted his head, his

insides were shaking with a need like he'd never felt before. "I want to make love to you, Maura."

Apparently his kiss had already told her what he wanted, because there wasn't so much as a flicker of surprise to be found on her face. Instead, her green eyes were dark and smoldering, telling him that she needed him just as badly. The notion left him drunk with anticipation.

"I want that, too, Quint."

He didn't question her a second time. He didn't want to give her the chance to change her mind, to turn away from him and the consequences this might bring upon them tomorrow. Loving her. Being inside her was all he could think about. It was all that mattered.

Groaning with need, he swept her up into his arms and carried her the few steps over to the cot. After lying her gently atop the blanket, he immediately joined her on the narrow mattress, then reached for her.

With a sigh that was lost in the sound of the rain, she moved into his arms and their lips united over and over in a swarm of kisses that grew deeper and bolder with each passing minute.

Eventually their clothing became an annoying barrier and Quint reached for the buttons on Maura's shirt. Once it was out of the way, he quickly followed it with her jeans and boots, then stood to deal with his own clothing.

Peeled down to nothing but two lacy scraps of lingerie, Maura sat on the side of the cot and as she watched Quint fumble with the buttons on his shirt, there was only one thing on her mind. And that thought had nothing to do with the right or wrong about making love to this man. Instead, she was wondering what he was thinking as he looked at her.

No doubt he was accustomed to having far younger women than her in his bed. And even though her body was firm and curved in all the right places, she felt self-conscious as his blue eyes slid slowly over her.

She swallowed as his jeans dropped to the floor, then tried to speak as he shoved them and his boots out of the way. He was all long, lean muscle, a man in the prime of his young life.

"I—" Heat bloomed pink on her cheeks as she unwittingly touched a hand to her messed hair. "I must look horrible," she said huskily. "I'm sorry…"

Groaning, he knelt before her and drew her into his arms. "Oh, hell, Maura. You're the most sexy and gorgeous woman I've ever laid eyes on."

Her head twisted back and forth against his bare shoulder. "There's no need for you to go overboard."

A low chuckle rumbled from deep in his throat. "I went overboard that first night I kissed you. I haven't been able to think of anything else since. I've been wondering, imagining how it would be to make love to you. And now—"

Cupping her face with both his hands, he looked into her eyes and Maura felt her heart swell with a longing that had nothing to do with physical desire and everything to do with an emotional bond.

"I don't want to make love to an athletic body, Maura. I want a flesh-and-blood woman, who's all soft and lovely and feels just right in my arms. I want you."

By the time he uttered the last word, his lips were against hers and Maura's doubts had flown through the cracks in the wall.

Quint wanted her. Really wanted her. And that in itself was enough to send her senses spinning, to make her forget everything, including the storm outside.

With his lips fastened hungrily to hers, he eased her back onto the cot, then stretched out beside her. Tiny shivers of pleasure raced down her spine as their bared skin touched, the heat of their bodies melded together and his hard arousal burgeoned between them.

Whirling in a foggy haze, the kiss continued until she was completely starving for air. Yet when he did finally tear his lips from hers, she wanted to cry at the loss. But her disappointment was short-lived as he quickly began to nibble at the sensitive spot beneath her ear, then followed that with a trail of moist kisses down the side of her neck.

By the time he reached the valley between her breasts, her fingers clenched against her palms and her body arched toward his, toward the mindless magic his mouth was playing across her skin.

One by one, he slipped the straps of her bra down her shoulders, unfastened the hooks, then tossed the garment to the floor.

She sucked in ragged breaths, while beneath a veil of lashes, she watched his gaze settle hungrily on her breasts. The desire raging in the pit of her belly twisted into a fiery ache and with a low groan, she clutched his shoulders and urged him down to her. Amidst the sound of the storm, she heard the sharp intake of his breath and then his mouth was against one nipple as he took the tight bud between his teeth and laved it with his tongue.

Inside Maura, something snapped like a twig and all the pent-up hunger she'd been trying to contain flooded through her like the downpour outside. Suddenly she couldn't touch him enough, taste him enough. Her hands raced over his hot skin, exploring the hard muscles of his arms and back while her lips scattered broken kisses along his collarbone and up the side of his neck where her mouth tasted the wild beat of his heart.

She was barely aware of him removing her panties and

his shorts. A sea of sensation was washing over her, tugging, smothering, begging, wiping away all sense of perception. And when he positioned himself above her, she reached for him with a fierceness that frightened her.

"I hope you're protected," he mouthed against her ear, "because I have nothing with me."

Closing her eyes, she turned her lips into the side of his face. "I am," she whispered, then with a choked groan, added, "I want to feel you inside me, Quint. I want to feel us together. That way."

"Oh, Maura. My lovely, lovely, Maura."

The raw huskiness in his voice, the tenderness in his blue eyes, pierced her chest and sank straight to her heart. Suddenly her throat was burning and her eyes were stinging, and before he could guess at the emotions he'd evoked in her, she buried her face against his chest and wrapped her arms tightly around him.

And when he entered her, the pleasure careening through her body was so great, so all-consuming that she was totally unaware of the stream of tears marking her cheeks.

## *Chapter Seven*

Much later, as Maura lay curled against Quint, her cheek pillowed by his chest, she listened to the even rhythm of his breathing, the slow beat of his heart, and knew they were sounds that would be with her for the rest of her life.

He'd taken her on a passionate trip the likes of which she'd never experienced. Even now, when she thought of how her whole body had exploded with pleasure, she was shocked and fascinated, dazed that he could have turned her into such a wild, uninhibited woman.

Oh, my, what had had happened? Making love to Quint had only shown her how much she'd done wrong. She'd not known that her ex-husband had been a selfish lover. Because Gil had been her first and only lover, she'd not had anyone to compare him to. But now, after Quint had touched her, lifted her to the sky and back, she realized she'd been missing so much, had wasted so many years on a one-sided relationship.

"I think the rain is letting up," Quint murmured against the top of her head. "But who cares? I could stay here all night. Just like this."

Moments ago, he'd pulled the Navajo blanket over them and now that the cooler air from the storm was filling the old storeroom, the warmth from the woven wool was welcome.

"Mmm. I'm thinking I could stay here forever," she said drowsily. "But something or someone would eventually show up to interrupt us."

She could feel his sigh ruffle her hair and then his hand was alongside her cheek, tilting her face up to his. When she looked into his blue eyes, her heart squeezed with bittersweet longing. Would he ever want to be with her again like this? Was she crazy to want to snatch what pleasure she could, whenever she could?

"Maura, before we leave here...I wanted you to know that this thing that's happened between us—I hadn't planned. Just in case you thought I'd calculated all this—"

He broke off as the upper part of her began to shake with soft chuckles.

"What's wrong?" he asked. "Am I funny or something?"

"Oh, Quint," she murmured, then scooting her whole body upward, she planted a kiss on his cheek. "For as long as I live, I would have never thought any such thing. You planning this with me? It's funny."

His expression sober, he arched one brow at her. "Really? What's so funny about it?"

Seeing he wasn't amused, she pressed her cheek against his. "I'm sorry if that didn't sound quite right. It's just that you—you can have any woman you want, Quint. The idea that you'd purposely pursue me is…well, ridiculous."

With his hands in her hair, he eased her face back from his. "Maura, I think I need to set your thinking straight about a few things. I'm not a playboy. I don't go after women."

"Of course not. You don't have to."

He groaned with frustration. "Okay, let me put it this way," he said. "Since the breakup with Holly, I've tried to date, to get interested in other women. And yes, I've had a few females deliberately try to catch my attention. But none of them sparked anything in me. Until now. Until you."

Could she believe him? Yes, she decided. Because he was talking about sexual desire, about that special spark of chemistry between a man and a woman. He wasn't talking about love. That was a whole other thing. A thing that he would never likely bring up. Nor would she.

Swallowing at the thickening in her throat, she said, "Then I'm very flattered, Quint, that you were attracted to me."

One corner of his rugged mouth turned upward. "And I'm very flattered that you wanted to get this close to me."

Her hand settled on the curve of his shoulder, then slipped down the hard, corded slope of his arm. Oh, yes, she thought, she wanted to be close to this man in a thousand, million ways.

"When you take a woman on a ride, you really take her on a ride," she teased softly.

He looked at her with faint disdain and then suddenly he was laughing, twisting her beneath him, and lowering his face down to hers. "You're good for me, Maura. You make me laugh. And that's not easy. Just ask Jake what I'm really like."

Her fingertip traced heart-shaped patterns upon his face. "I'd rather ask you."

He looked at her, his eyes gliding hungrily over her flushed cheeks and swollen lips, the tangled hair hiding one green eye.

"I'm not an easy man to like, Maura. I'm quiet and moody. And small talk mostly bores me. I'd rather be with my horses. I don't particularly like money and I hate crowds."

Her lips curved into a sexy little purse. "Mmm. You sound like a terrible sort of man. Anything else I should know?"

"Yeah. I don't know anything about being romantic and even if I did, I wouldn't bother."

"Why?"

"Because romance is looking at the world through rose-colored glasses. And when a woman looks at me, I want her to clearly see the flaws she'd be getting."

In order to keep her away? Maura decided the answer to that question didn't matter. She was looking at him and the future with clear eyes. Quint was a straightforward guy. She'd gone into his arms knowing not to pin any sort of hopes and dreams on the two of them being together permanently.

"Don't worry," she replied. "I won't be expecting flowers."

He stared at her for long moments and then his mouth crushed down on hers in a kiss that wiped everything from her mind and stirred the want in her all over again.

"Maybe we'd better stay here a little longer," he whispered huskily. "Until the rain stops."

Almost a week later, Quint found himself driving up the narrow dirt road that led to his grandfather's ranch house.

For the past few days, he'd fought the urge to return to Apache Wells. He didn't have the time or energy to make the forty-mile drive often. Hell, he didn't need to remind himself that he had a ranch of his own to run. With cattle to buy, fences to build, feeders to erect and horses to move from the Chaparral to the Golden Spur, he hardly had time to draw a good breath. But here he was anyway, he thought wryly. Because, in spite of his work and exhaustion, he desperately wanted to see Maura again.

Maura. With her wine-red hair and sea-green eyes. She'd bewitched him. That's what she'd done. He could scarcely close his eyes without thinking of her naked, her hips arching up to his, scattering his senses like bits of grass in the wind. He'd expected to enjoy making love to her. After all, she was pretty and sexy; a combination hard for any man to resist. But he'd also expected the incident to be a brief encounter to enjoy for the moment, then sweep entirely from his mind.

*Face it, Quint. The woman turned you inside out. She shot you straight to heaven, then let you fall back to earth with the slow rocking motion of a drifting feather. You'd never felt anything like it. And now you're beginning to wonder if she's something special. The sex was special, you fool. Not her. Get over it.*

The cynical voice that had followed Quint around for the last six years tormented him until he braked his truck to a halt in front of the house and climbed out. Yeah, it probably was pure sex that had pushed him to drive forty miles this evening when he should have been taking an early night at home, he thought. But what was wrong with that? He was a man after all. And a man had needs.

To his surprise, he found Abe in his recliner, the television off and a Bible lying open on his lap. Maura wasn't anywhere to be seen.

"Hey, Gramps," he greeted.

Looking up with surprise, Abe carefully folded the book together. "Well," he said mockingly, "the long-lost grandson has finally decided to honor me with a visit."

Quint grimaced. "Don't give me that bull. I was just over here last week. You expect me to come over here and hold your hand every day?"

Abe wiped a hand over his drooping white mustache. "No. After one or two days your smart lip would get mighty tryin'," he countered.

Quint took a seat on the end of the couch, while looking and listening for signs of Maura. The house seemed exceptionally quiet and he couldn't smell any sort of cooking coming from the kitchen.

"What are you doing in the house?" Quint asked him. "I thought you'd be down at the bunkhouse, playing cards with Jim and having coffee."

"If you thought that, what are you doing in the house?" Abe parried.

Quint was shocked to feel his face flushing with heat. There was no point for him to hide his interest in Maura. Abe was too crafty for that. "I wanted to talk to Maura."

"Well, you should have called first. She ain't here."

Quint had called three days ago. His conversation with Maura had been pleasant but brief, during which he'd told her he'd see her in a few days. The few days were up and here he was feeling like an idiot for presuming she'd be sitting around his grandfather's ranch, waiting for him to make an appearance.

"Where is she?"

Abe placed the Bible on the end table next to his chair. "She's at the hospital."

It was all Quint could do to keep from leaping to his

feet. "Hospital! Has something happened to her? And you didn't call me?"

Beneath his bushy brows, Abe leveled a disgusted look at him. "Hell, boy, if something was wrong with Maura you think I'd be sitting here?"

Relief pouring through him, Quint rubbed his palms down his thighs. "No," he conceded gruffly, "I guess not."

"Damn right I wouldn't," Abe stormed back at him. "I'd be right by her side. That's how a man shows his love."

Caught by those last words, Quint's brows arched with dismay. "You love Maura?"

Abe snorted as though Quint's question was absurd. "Of course I love her. I've loved her from the first moment I laid eyes on her."

Hell. That's exactly what Quint had feared all along. "I see."

"No, damn it, you don't see. You haven't seen much of anything about women since that silly little Johnson gal threw you over the fence for another man. You think they're all like her, that they've all got their claws out for you. Well, if you'd take the time to look, you'd see that Maura doesn't have any claws. That's one of the reasons I love her."

Dear God, Quint hadn't driven for nearly an hour to get this sort of preaching, to hear his grandfather admit that he loved the same woman that Quint had taken to his bed. This was insanity.

"Okay. You've made your point, Gramps," he said wearily. "You're in love with the woman and I should realize that she's an angel."

Abe's boots banged loudly against the footrest as he positioned the chair upright and got to his feet. "Quint, I didn't say I was 'in' love with Maura. I said I loved her.

There's a difference. Sometimes a man has to know his limitations and I can see that she's too young for me. So," he said with a shrug, "I just have to settle with havin' her company. Until she gets tangled up with a man who'll give her a family."

Quint let out a pent-up breath. "She's told you that she wants a family?"

"Not in so many words. But I can just tell when a woman is ripe for that sort of thing."

If that was the case, then Abe knew a hell of a lot more than Quint knew. From what Maura had implied to him, she wasn't ready to jump into a serious situation with any man. That was one of the reasons Quint had been drawn to her in the first place. He didn't have to worry about her getting all clingy and demanding.

"Tell me, Gramps, did Granny know that you were such an expert on women?"

"'Course she did. She taught me everything I know." He motioned for Quint to follow him to the kitchen. "C'mon. Let's find us something to eat. And maybe Maura will show up before long."

A few minutes later, when Maura arrived and spotted Quint's truck parked near the front gate, her heart leaped into a dizzying speed. Even though darkness had just now settled over the ranch, daylight savings time made the hour late. Had he made the long drive to see his grandfather? Or her?

After parking her car beneath a covered carport at the back, she entered the house through the kitchen door and discovered both men sitting at the table, eating leftovers from the day before.

As soon as Quint spotted her, he immediately rose to

his feet and Maura felt something melt inside as her gaze connected with his blue eyes.

"Come sit with us, Maura," he invited. "Gramps was just telling me that Brady was involved in some sort of scrape."

Brady was Maura's youngest brother had worked as the chief deputy to Lincoln County's sheriff, Ethan Hamilton. Earlier this afternoon, when Maura had gotten the call that he'd been wounded, she'd left the ranch at breakneck speed and with a litany of prayers passing her lips, sped to the hospital. The ordeal had drained her, but now, seeing Quint was refueling her with happy pleasure.

Shoving a hand through her hair, she pushed the disheveled strands away from her face. "Yes, unfortunately. Some of the men in the department had set up a drug sting and things went amiss when one of the dealers smelled a rat. He pulled out a gun and began shooting. Brady's arm was hit with a small caliber bullet, but thankfully it was a flesh wound and should heal in a short time."

She walked over to the table, where Quint already had a chair pulled out for her. As he helped her into it, his closeness shook her, reminded her that she'd spent the past several nights lying awake thinking about him and the way he'd made love to her in such a thorough, precious way.

"That's good to hear," Abe said. "Lord knows that brother of yours earns his money the hard way."

Maura smiled at the old man. "Being a deputy is what he loves to do. Like I love nursing you." She reached across the table and squeezed his hand. "Have you been feeling okay while I was gone?"

He grinned at her. "If I felt any better I'd have to go out

and jump a fence. And Quint here showed up to keep me company. That's somethin' that don't happen every day."

At the opposite end of the table, Quint cleared his throat. "We were just having a little supper, Maura. Would you like a plate? Something to drink?" he asked.

She wanted none of those things. She simply wanted to be in his arms, to feel herself all wrapped up against his hard body, his lips moving against hers. Oh my, oh my, what had this man done to her? She was sex-crazed, but only one certain man would do.

"No thanks. Before I left the hospital, I had something with Bridget and my grandmother."

"Kate was there?" Abe asked with surprise.

Maura smiled to herself. From time to time Abe had brought up the subject of Maura's grandmother, Kate. It was obvious he was interested in the woman, but she doubted he'd ever admit it, especially to Kate. If anything, Kate was even bolder spoken than Abe. Sparks would fly if the two of them ever got together.

"Dad couldn't keep her away. She's always been especially close to Brady. Maybe because he's the baby and much more like her than any of us. But everything is under control and when I left the hospital the rest of my family were heading for home."

"That's good," Abe said, then abruptly rose to his feet. "Well, that's about all I can eat right now. I'm gonna head down to the bunkhouse and see if Jim's up to a game of poker. Damn man skinned me for thirty dollars last night. I gotta win it back."

"It's dark outside," Quint warned him. "You'd better drive."

"I know how to get to my own bunkhouse," he muttered as he disappeared out the door.

Bemused by the old man's quick departure, Quint said, "What's wrong with him? He always wants coffee after he eats."

"From what he tells me, Jim always keeps a pot going on the stove," Maura reasoned.

"Well, the way he scooted out of here, you'd think he wanted to leave us alone," Quint said, then leveled a suggestive look at her. "What do you think?"

Heat swept through her body, making it feel like her cotton dress was actually a heavy woolen coat. Refraining from fanning herself, she rose to her feet and began to gather Abe's dirty dishes.

"Clearly," she said as she carried the things over to the sink.

Not bothering with his own dishes, Quint left the table and walked up behind her. As he slipped his arms around her waist and pressed his lips to the back of her neck, he said in a voice muffled by her skin, "I think the old man needs psychotherapy. He says he loves you."

She didn't so much as flinch. Instead, she asked, "Are you saying a man has to be mentally ill to love me?"

The coolness in her voice told him he'd gone at this all wrong. "No. But Gramps is eighty-four."

"So. You don't think you'll be capable of loving at eighty-four?"

Hell, he wasn't sure he was capable of loving a woman at twenty-nine, he thought. These past years since his break with Holly he'd tried to get close to other women, tried to recapture that blissful state of mind he'd had with his first sweetheart. But the most he'd experienced was a cold sweat, a sick repulsion at the idea of handing any woman the reins to his future.

Quint figured by the time he reached Abe's age, his

heart would more than likely be as hard as a piece of granite. Maybe it was now, he thought bitterly. Maybe Holly had turned him to stone and he'd never be able to love again.

Lifting his head, he answered, "Not a woman fifty years my junior!"

Twisting around, she slipped her arms around his midsection and linked her hands behind his back. "Oh, Quint," she said with a soft laugh, "Abe loves me as a daughter."

Her laughter was all he needed to lighten his thoughts and he smiled at her. "I suppose you're right. I just don't want his old heart broken."

As for his own heart, Quint wasn't worried about that. After all, a piece of rock wasn't capable of getting all soft and soppy and vulnerable.

"I was surprised to see you here tonight," she said huskily.

"Why? I told you on the phone that I'd see you soon."

The husky note in his voice sent a shiver of anticipation down Maura's spine. "That could mean anything. And you've been very busy."

"Jake and I have finally started stocking the ranch and for the past week, we've been moving cattle and horses from dawn 'til dusk. I've hardly taken time to eat." His hands gently framed her face. "But—oh, honey, you ought to know I've been going crazy to be with you again."

She sighed. "I've been wanting to see you again, too."

He bent his head and his lips wrapped desperately over hers. The force of his kiss rocked her head backward and she moaned as her hands reached for the anchor of his shoulders.

In spite of the overhead lighting, his kiss was tugging her down into a swirling darkness where there was nothing but his hands sizzling over her skin, his mouth demanding, yet at the same time giving.

When their lips finally broke apart and his forehead was resting against hers, she sucked in ragged breaths and attempted to calm her racing heart.

"This is crazy, Quint!"

"Yeah. But a good kind of crazy."

He pressed his lips across her forehead, then along one cheekbone, while goose bumps danced over Maura's skin.

"The way I want you is indecent," she whispered. "You shouldn't be making me feel like this."

Her head tilted sideways as his lips began a downward trail on the side of her neck, then paused against the throbbing vein at the juncture of her shoulder.

"I've got to make love to you, Maura."

"Yes…" The word floated out on a sigh.

His lips began working their way back up her throat and toward her lips. Aching with need, Maura's hips shamelessly arched into his.

"Not here—not in your grandfather's house," she uttered with dismay.

Groaning with frustration, he dipped his hand beneath the hem of her skirt, then glided his hand up her thigh until his fingers reached the silky fabric of her panties. While he teased the flesh of one buttock, he whispered, "Gramps will be gone for hours."

Knowing that she couldn't succumb to his seductive persuasions on this matter, she purposely pushed at his shoulders to wedge a few cooling inches between them. "Maybe. Maybe not. It doesn't matter. I wouldn't feel right."

Seeing she meant what she said, Quint grabbed her hand and began tugging her toward the door. "C'mon. I know somewhere we can go."

"Go? Now?" she asked dazedly. "Where?"

"You'll see. It's not far."

Unable to resist, Maura allowed him to lead her outside to the front of the house, where he quickly helped her into the cab of his truck. As he pulled away from the ranch house, a sense of reckless anticipation came over her and she looked at him as though they'd suddenly turned into sneaky partners in crime.

"What if Abe returns to the house and finds us gone? What are we going to tell him?"

Quint chuckled. "That I took you sightseeing."

Maura groaned with misgiving. "In the dark? The man isn't that ancient, Quint."

"Does it matter what he thinks?"

He reached across the seat for her hand and as his fingers closed around hers, she could feel her heart throbbing with excitement. What normal woman wouldn't thrill at the idea of her lover carrying her off in the dark to a secret hideaway?

"No," she whispered truthfully. "It can't matter."

About two miles from the house, he turned onto a dim dirt road that led north toward the mountains. During her morning jogs, Maura had noticed the road, but never explored it.

"Are we still on Apache Wells?" she asked after he'd driven for another five minutes.

By now the road had grown bumpy and a dense pine forest had narrowed the road down to the width of a single vehicle. As the truck climbed the rough terrain, Maura gripped the seat in order to steady herself.

"Honey, you have to drive ten miles back to the main highway before you're off of Apache Wells."

"I wasn't sure. We're going toward the mountains. And it doesn't look like anyone travels this road very often."

"Only me. And if any cattle go astray, the ranch hands might use it. But that's rare."

She was peering out the windshield, wondering how much farther the truck could handle the rough terrain when suddenly the road planed out, and straight ahead, in the beam of the headlights, stood a small log cabin embraced by a stand of tall pines.

Quint quickly stopped the truck, then helped her to ground. As they walked toward the entrance, their footsteps made silent by pine needles, Maura got the sense that the structure was old. Possibly even older than the ranch itself.

Using his shoulder, Quint shoved the door inward, then ordered her to stay put until he provided light.

Standing in the doorway, the cool night air to her back and the silence of the woods surrounding them, a brief moment of stark sanity raced through her mind.

What was she doing here? With a man younger than her and definitely far less committed? Had she lost her senses and thrown every scrap of self-respect to the wind?

Commitment. Self-respect. She'd had those things before. Or so she'd believed. They had brought her nothing but heartache. Being with Quint brought her joy. And no matter how short-lived that joy was she was going to take it, savor it and be glad for it.

After Quint lit a kerosene lantern and a fat candle, he motioned for Maura to enter the small, one-room cabin. As she stepped onto the bare, wooden floor and glanced around at the crude fixtures, he said, "It's a little dusty. But not bad. I'll open the windows and that should give us some fresh air."

At the front of the room, Quint unlatched two wooden squares that pushed outward to create window spaces.

After he'd securely propped them and the cool night air rushed in, he walked back to where she stood by a tiny table holding the burning lamp.

"Alone. At last," he said with a growl of satisfaction.

Maura's heart leaped to a reckless speed as his hands settled at the sides of her waist. "You've taken a lot of trouble to get me up here," she said huskily.

In the dim glow of the lamp, she watched his gaze travel straight to her swollen lips and her loins clenched with desire.

"And you're worth every minute of it."

He was not a man to hand her lines and as he pulled her into his arms, she wondered if he'd actually meant the words he'd whispered.

*Don't go trying to figure the man now, Maura. Just remember this time with him isn't forever and you'll be okay.*

Closing her eyes, she turned her lips up to his and as his kiss swept her into a vortex of pleasures she forgot about his motives and plans or the condition her heart might be in tomorrow. Tonight was all about him and her being together and nothing else.

Before long he was removing her clothing and carrying her to a built-in bunk spread with a down comforter. From the small bed, she watched him undress in the dim yellow glow of the lamplight and as the soft shadows slipped fingers across his hard body, her throat thickened with emotions she didn't understand or even want to analyze.

This amazing man wanted her. Needed her. That was enough for now.

At Chillicothe, she'd believed it impossible for Quint to thrill her more, to take her to even higher heights with his lovemaking, but somehow he did and it was a long time afterward before she could find the strength or composure to utter a word.

Lying in his arms, her body lax and replete, she rested her cheek upon his shoulder and savored the feel of his fingertips marking a gentle trail from her hip to her breast and back again.

"What is this place?" she asked drowsily.

"Our hideaway," he murmured.

By now the candle had burned out and the single flame of the lamp mottled the chinked walls with golden splashes of light. Beyond the open windows and above the tops of the pines, she could see a portion of the black sky riddled with stars and at that moment it was impossible to think of a more beautiful place to be.

Her lips tilted to a dreamy smile. "I mean before."

"The cabin was here before Gramps built the ranch and we figured pioneers must have lived here long ago. At one time Gramps used it as a hunting cabin. But now he'd rather feed the deer than shoot them. And so do I."

"Do you come here often?"

He shifted ever so slightly, and then she felt his lips brushing against the crown of her hair. It was such a sweet and loving contact that her throat suddenly stung with tears.

"No. The last time I was here was more than a year ago, when I learned that my mother had kept a secret life from me and my sister, Alexa."

"I heard bits and pieces about that even before I returned to Hondo Valley. Knowing your lovely mother, it's still hard for me to imagine her having another family that no one knew about."

He sighed and Maura could only imagine what the ordeal with Frankie Cantrell had done to him. It hurt to think of him going through such emotional turmoil. Like her, everything he'd believed in had been ripped asunder and she knew firsthand the deep wounds that deception left behind.

"No one knew about her first marriage but my father," he said lowly. "And he took the secret to his grave. Seems my parents decided that it would be too hard on Alexa and me to know that we had brothers in Texas, but couldn't associate with them. You see, Mom's first husband was abusive. She was forced to run from him and didn't stop running until she reached Ruidoso. He must have been a real bastard. On the other hand there must have been some good in the man because my two half brothers are great guys."

She smoothed her palm across his broad chest. "You get along with them?"

"Oh, sure. Why do you ask? Did you think I might resent them?"

"It would be only natural to feel resentment. Especially since Abe told me that your mother makes regular trips to Texas to see them."

His hand lifted from her hip and then his fingers pushed into her long hair to lift the strands away from her cheek and neck.

"I'd never be jealous of that. Mac and Ripp have families and she needs to be a part of their lives. She missed out on so much. And Alexa lives there now, too. So she has plenty of reasons to go there often."

"You ever get the itch to move closer to your siblings?" she asked thoughtfully.

"Move from New Mexico? Away from Gramps? Never. This land is a part of my soul. And Gramps is—well, ever since I've been big enough to walk, he's been my hero."

With a throaty groan, he rolled her onto her back and poised his lips over hers. "Besides, if I moved to Texas, you'd have to come up here to the cabin by yourself. And that wouldn't be any fun at all."

No. Life without Quint would be boring and lonely, Maura thought. It was something she refused to think about. At least, for tonight.

"How lucky for me that you're not a wanderer," she murmured, then latching her fingers around the back of his neck, she pulled his head down to hers and closed the last bit of space between their lips.

*Chapter Eight*

Two weeks later Maura stared numbly across the desk at her sister. It was past the clinic's normal working hours and the last of Bridget's patients had left the building. All except Maura.

"What did you say?" Maura asked in a slow, dazed voice.

Her hands folded in front of her, Bridget leaned forward and in her no-nonsense manner, repeated, "I said you're not suffering from an acid stomach. You're going to have a baby. I'd say in about eight months from now."

"A baby! How—how can…that be?"

Bridget smiled knowingly. "You meet a man, chemistry clicks and before you know it the two of you are too close for comfort."

With a loud wail, Maura's head shook back and forth. "That's not what I mean! I'm talking about birth control! How did it fail? All those years with Gil—"

"Yeah. Thank God it didn't fail with him," Bridget muttered, then smiled at Maura as though she couldn't be happier. "I suspect you unwittingly forgot a pill or two. Or it could be the dosage needs to be changed. In any case, do not take another one."

Dropping her head in her hand, Maura struggled to think past the shock of the moment to the past month or two, before she'd fallen into bed with Quint Cantrell. "Now that I think about it, I did get fouled up for a few days. That's when Dr. Weston was hounding me and I'd given the hospital notice to quit my job. I guess with all the stress I forgot to take a few pills. But I got back on schedule more than six weeks ago."

Bridget shook her head. "Apparently the interruption was enough to give your reproductive organs a window of opportunity. And they took it."

Oh, God. How was she going to explain this to Quint? How on earth was he going to react to the news that he was going to be a father?

Trembling now, she rose from the wooden chair and began to pace around the small space of Bridget's office.

"Oh, Brita, this is unbelievable! What am I going to do?"

Bridget's brows arched with faint surprise. "Why, Maura, there shouldn't be a question with you. You're going to have the baby."

Stopping in her tracks, Maura bit back a yell of frustration. "Of course there's no question about that! Every cell in my body loves and wants this baby. I was talking about the father! He—he is not going to be pleased. In fact, I figure he's going to be outraged."

Frowning with doubt, Bridget asked, "How do you know that? I've always thought of Quint as a sensible, responsible person. At least that's how I always saw him in high school. 'Course I can't say much for him hanging on to that gold-digging Holly like he did. But I forgive him because he was young and it takes a man longer to wise up about life. I'll bet after all this time he can see what a narrow escape he made with that witch."

Stunned, Maura stared at her. "How did you know the father was Quint? I haven't told you anything about seeing him and—"

A sly smile spread across Bridget's face. "I'm not blind. I'm your sister. And I've been seeing the change in you since you went to work for old Abe. Then that night at the hospital, when Brady was there with the gunshot wound, I overheard you telling Dr. Weston, in no uncertain terms, to get lost and stay lost. I knew then that you'd finally woken up and come out of your shell. And I figured Quint had to be reason. Abe is certainly too old to bring about that sort of change in you."

Groaning with embarrassment, Maura covered her face with her hands. "Oh, Lord, you must be thinking I've lost my mind. He's so young and—"

"A hunk to boot," Bridget finished for her, then let out a suggestive laugh. "I think for the first time ever, my sister has really blossomed into the woman she should be. And Maura, just think, you're going to have a child! Finally! Oh, how I envy you!"

Completely dismayed, Maura walked back over to Bridget's desk. "Envy me? Are you crazy? I'm divorced, single and pregnant. With a child whose father doesn't love me. I'm sure you'd jump at the chance to trade places with me."

Bridget shook her curly head. "How do you know Quint doesn't love you? Has he told you that?"

Maura's troubled gaze dropped to the floor. "No. But he doesn't have to. What we have—it's like you said a few moments ago. Just chemistry."

"So you don't love him, either? That's strange because I just can't imagine my big sister jumping into bed with a man she doesn't care about. Really care about."

Did she love Quint? For the past few weeks she'd been telling herself that her heart hadn't taken that big of leap for the man, but deep down she had to admit she'd only been fooling herself. She was wild about him. Crazy about him. She couldn't imagine life without him. If that meant she loved him, then she was definitely guilty.

"So maybe I do care about him," she muttered. "Maybe I do love him. That doesn't fix anything. He doesn't love me back. And he sure as heck doesn't want to get married."

Sighing, Bridget reached for a prescription pad and began to scribble instructions on it. "Maura; you need to remember you're not dealing with Gilbert anymore. Quint is a real man. Not a jerk."

Standing, she moved around the desk and handed the scrap of paper to her sister. "Here's a script for vitamins and something for your stomach. Take them all faithfully and try to eat right. Right now that little one's most important parts are developing. We want him to be healthy whenever he gets here. Or maybe it's a she," Bridget added with a happy grin. "I can't wait to see! Are you going to tell the family, or can I break the news?"

Maura's mouth fell open. She'd not yet thought about her parents' reaction to this news, or her other siblings. She'd always been the cautious, practical Donovan. Were they now going to see her as disgrace to the family?

"Don't say anything just yet. I need a few days to come to terms with all of this and gather my wits about me. I'm not sure I can face anyone with the news right now. Especially Quint. And he needs to hear this first."

A few minutes later as she left Bridget's office, Maura began to doubt the wisdom of holding her secret for a few more days. The longer she held this sort of news from Quint, the worse it would make things. Especially if Bridget accidentally let it slip to her family and the information got back to him before Maura had a chance to speak with him.

The thought of confronting Quint with this sort of life-changing news was twisting her nerves into knots and yet in spite of that, she was euphoric, thrilled to her very toes at the idea of a tiny life growing inside of her.

For years now she'd had to push aside her desire for a child. And after the humiliating divorce with Gilbert, she'd practically crossed out the idea that she'd ever be a mother. But now a baby was actually growing inside of her. Quint's baby! As far as she was concerned, it was a miraculous turn of events.

Nearly an hour later, when she parked in front of Abe's house, her mind was still spinning as she tried to decide how to approach Quint.

This past Sunday, she'd had a brief phone call from him, explaining that he and Jake were leaving for Clovis on Monday morning and weren't planning to be back until Wednesday, which was today. The trip was to purchase a special herd of cattle and haul them back to the Golden Spur. Calling him tonight wouldn't be the wise thing to do, she decided, as she let herself into the house.

No doubt he'd be tired and could possibly still be out on the range, moving the cattle to their new location. When she talked to him about the baby, she wanted his undivided attention. Early in the morning, before he became too deeply involved in work, she'd call and suggest they meet somewhere private. He'd probably get the idea that she was calling to make a date for them to make love. And he'd be partly right, she thought wryly.

"Maura, is that you, honey?"

Maura turned from putting her purse away to see Abe entering the living room. The look of concern on his face troubled her even more than she was already. She was here to see after Abe's health. Not the other way around. But several times this past week he'd caught her taking stomach medication instead of eating her breakfast and he'd pestered her until she'd promised to drive to town and visit the doctor.

Smoothing a hand over her hair, she wondered if she looked as unsettled as she felt. "I'm sorry I'm so late getting back, Abe. My sister was very busy and had to work me in as her last patient."

"Hmmph," he said with a snort. "You'd think being a relative you'd get special treatment."

"Bridget always plays fair," she said, then looked at him more closely. "Are you feeling okay?"

"Hell, yeah! Just worried about you." He took her by the arm and led through the small hallway toward the kitchen. "I've fixed you a nice little supper and I want you to sit and eat."

"Abe—"

"It's soup and crackers and iced tea. It'll soothe your stomach," he insisted.

Her heart melted. Abe wasn't a kitchen person. For him to take this much trouble for her was more than touching.

"Okay, I'll try to eat a little," she told him. "Let me go wash up and I'll be right back."

After a quick trip to the bathroom, Maura headed to the

kitchen and found Abe at the cookstove. As she sidled up to him, he winked at her and she suddenly realized that no matter what happened with Quint, she would always have this man's love. It was a comforting thought.

Stirring the broth and noodles, he explained, "Just giving the soup a little heat. Did that sister of yours give you something to fix your stomach?"

Maura let out a heavy breath. "Sort of."

Scowling, he practically shouted, "What the hell does that mean? Can't she fix an upset stomach? You need to eat. You're lookin' gaunt."

Emotions clogged her throat and stung her eyes. She tried to push it all away, but it was like fighting a tidal wave. Joy and fear were carrying on a giant war inside of her and she didn't know how to make the two emotions call a truce.

"I'll be fine," she said hoarsely. "It's just going to take a while for me to get over this."

Lying the spoon to one side, he thoughtfully ran his fingers down his drooping mustache, then cut his sharp gaze directly to her face.

"Why is that? You gonna have a baby?"

Maura gasped as warm color flooded her cheeks. "How did you guess?"

He grinned as though she'd just handed him a box of prized treasure. "My missus was pregnant twice. The first one she lost. The next one was Lewis. Both times she couldn't eat and she had that look about her. The same one you have now."

Maura's hands flew to her face. "Oh, Abe," she said with a tortured groan. "This is— I wasn't expecting this to happen to me. And I'm so happy. But I'm scared, too. I don't know what to think or what to do."

Horrified that she was going to cry in front of the old man, she bent her head and desperately tried to blink away the tears. As she tried to collect herself, she felt Abe's bony hands wrapping around her shoulders and pulling her into the circle of his arms.

"Maura, honey, this ain't anything to cry about. This is a wonderful thing. Really wonderful."

Resting her cheek against his shoulder, she sniffed. "You think so?"

Chuckles rumbled deep in his chest and the sound comforted Maura somewhat. If only Quint would react this way, she thought, then everything would be okay.

"God has blessed you. How can anything be bad about that?"

Lifting her head, she gave him a watery smile. "You're right. Babies are a gift," she agreed. "Even when they aren't planned."

"Now you're talkin' like my Maura girl." Patting her back, he leaned forward and pecked a kiss on her cheek. "Congratulations!"

Maura was giving the old man a grateful hug, when out of the blue Quint's voice sounded from across the room.

"Gramps? What—"

Turning away from Abe, she watched Quint saunter into the room. He looked tired and dusty and totally astounded as his squinted gaze vacillated between her and his grandfather.

Abe made a production of clearing his throat, then turned and switched off the fire beneath the copper saucepan.

"Looks like things are heated enough," he said in an overly loud voice. "You'd better take care of things now, Maura. I've got a date with the poker table."

The old man started out of the room, while a dumbfounded Quint stared after him. "Gramps! What are you doing? I—"

"Makin' myself scarce. That's what I'm doing," Abe interrupted. Then pausing at the door, he scowled at his grandson. "Make yourself at home, son. You always do."

Abe left the house, the screen door banging behind him. Quint immediately whirled on Maura for an explanation.

"What's the matter with him? And why was he kissing you? And why do you look so— What's happened around here?"

Closing her eyes, she breathed deeply and tried to compose herself. She wasn't ready for this. She needed more time to make a plan, to think of the best way to tell him he was going to be a daddy. But the moment Quint had walked into the room, all time had been snatched away from her.

"Abe's okay. He was trying to comfort me. Because… because—"

She couldn't finish and Quint crossed the room to where she stood, only to stop in his tracks when he spotted the damp trail of tears on her cheeks.

"You've been crying!" he exclaimed. "What's happened? Brady? He's not been wounded again, has he?"

Her stomach was fluttering, her heart racing madly. "No, my brother is fine. As far as I know everything with my family is okay. I've been a bit under the weather the past few days and—"

Uneasy now, he closed the last bit of space between them and wrapped his arms around her waist. "You didn't sound ill whenever I called you Sunday evening. You didn't mention anything to me then about being sick."

"No. I didn't know then what I know now."

A puzzled frown wrinkled his forehead. "You're not making sense."

Quint watched her wipe a shaky hand over her face and then she wrapped a hand around his arm and urged him toward the table. Like a lost lamb, he followed, his heart sinking with each step he took.

"I'm feeling a little shaky," she said. "While I explain, I need to sit. You need to sit."

Explain what? he wondered wildly. That she had some sort of terminal disease? That her days were numbered? The mere idea that he might lose her for any reason shook him right down to the heels of his boots. How, when had this woman come to mean so much to him? How had he let it happen?

"Maura, are you seriously ill? Tell me—"

At the head of the small dining table, she practically pushed him down in the chair, then sank limply in the one next to him.

Quint reached for her hand and squeezed it tightly. He needed to hold on to her. He needed to reassure himself that she was still the same vibrant woman he'd made love to in the hunting cabin.

"Please, Quint, this is nothing to worry about," she said quickly, trying to allay his fears. Then with a soft sigh she glanced to a spot across the room. "This is not the way I'd planned to do this. I wanted us to be in a nice, quiet place—somewhere special. I wanted you to be in a good mood and—"

"I am in a good mood. And Gramps's kitchen has always been a special place to me."

A faint smile touched her lips. "Maybe so. But you're frowning and nervous," she pointed out.

"Because you're making me that way with all this dallying around!" he said in a raised voice. "And you still haven't entirely explained why Gramps needed to comfort you with a kiss and a bear hug. Does he think that sort of stuff is going to heal you?"

Her nostrils flared and Quint could only think how beautiful she was when she was lying beneath him, her lips parted, her green eyes begging him to make love to her. He'd never had a woman who could weaken him with just a look. Until now.

"He wasn't trying to heal me," she said drolly. "He was congratulating me."

Seeing she was trying to make light of things, he teased, "For what? Keeping those dizzy rocks out of his ears?"

"No!" she wailed. Then she heaved out a heavy breath and turned her green eyes directly on his searching gaze. "Because I'm going to have a baby."

Quint didn't know how it happened, but suddenly his chair was teetering backward and he was in danger of hitting the hard tiled floor.

After scrambling to right himself, he stared at her in stunned fascination. "A—baby! How can that be? Are you sure?"

Nodding, she looked at him, her expression grim. "My sister ran a test. It's very accurate."

Momentarily paralyzed with shock, he tried to form the questions rushing at him like a hail of bullets. A baby! Him, a father! It was incredible! "But it's only been… It's not been that long since we… And you said you were on the pill!"

She closed her eyes and as he watched her bosom rapidly rise and fall, it suddenly dawned on him that she'd been crying because of the baby. Did that mean she didn't want it? That she'd told his grandfather about the pregnancy before she'd even bothered to tell him? Oh, God, what was going on in his lover's head? And why did everything in the room seem to be spinning around him as though he were drunk?

"Nowadays medical tests can tell when a woman is only a few days pregnant. Bridget estimates I'm three to four weeks along. So that means our trip to Chillicothe produced more than just a rainstorm," she said, then sucked in a deep breath and went on before Quint had time to digest half of her words. "As far as the birth control— that's a little harder to explain."

"Try."

Her lips pursed as she raked her eyes over his face and Quint realized he wasn't handling this in a sensitive enough way to suit her. But damn it, she'd shocked the hell out of him. And he wasn't a flowery man. She might as well get used to that and a whole lot more. Because it looked like their lives were about to drastically change.

Rising from the chair, she began to wander aimlessly around the small kitchen. Quint's gaze followed her slender figure while a wondrous sort of realization struck him. His baby was growing inside of her! A son. A daughter. And he wanted it as much as he wanted to draw his next breath.

She said, "A month before…uh…you and I…er…had sex, I got fouled up on my pill schedule. I didn't miss any, but they weren't taken in the proper succession. At the time I didn't think much about it. I mean since Gil I haven't been near a man. And when you…when we were together I'd long forgotten about getting out of sync with my pills."

Something inside of Quint suddenly wanted to shout out a joyous hallelujah. Yet at the same time icy shards of fear were splintering through him. How could he be so mixed up? How could he feel happy and terrified at the same time?

When he finally spoke, the tightness of his throat made his voice hoarse. "I see. So you told Abe about the baby before you bothered to even tell me."

Her pacing stopped and when she looked at him, her eyes flickered with uncertainty. What was she expecting him to do, throw a walleyed fit or something even more violent? The idea tore at him, made him realize that in spite of their lovemaking, she didn't know him as a man. Not as he wanted her to know him.

"I didn't run to Abe with the news, if that's what you're thinking," she answered. "Before I ever went to see Bridget, Abe was aware that I'd been feeling poorly and he guessed I was pregnant. I could hardly lie and deny it, Quint."

Rising to his feet, he went to her and gathered her hands in his. In spite of the connection, she continued to look up at him, her eyes searching, waiting, wanting. What was she expecting from him? And whatever it was, would he be able to give it to her?

"I should have known," he said gently. "The old man seems to have an inside line to God."

"Well—I can safely say your grandfather was happy about the news." Her troubled gaze dropped to the middle of his chest. "But I feel very badly, Quint. It's my fault that the birth control didn't work. And me being a nurse, I should have known—remembered about the pills and realized there could be a problem. But I— Well, that day at Chillicothe I wasn't thinking straight."

And that day his mind had stopped working completely, Quint realized. Even if she'd told him there was a chance she might get pregnant, he would have made love to her anyway. He'd wanted her that much.

His fingers tightened around hers. "No one is at fault, Maura. We did this together."

Her gaze lifted up to his and then a long breath eased out of her as though he'd just released a heavy yoke from around her neck. "Thank you, Quint," she said lowly. "I didn't want you to think… Well, I don't want you to feel obligated or—or cornered. I mean, I'll be happy for you to be all the father you want to be. But if you don't, I'll understand, too. After all, it's not like…we're madly in love or…engaged…or anything. And this all happened quite by accident."

As Maura spoke there were so many emotions erupting inside Quint that he couldn't describe any of them, much less understand why he was feeling them. The only thing he was able to disentangle from the messy turmoil was the sudden burst of anger shooting straight to the top of his head.

Dropping her hands, he repeated with cool amazement, "Cornered? Obligated? Do you realize how you sound? You're talking about my child. Mine! Everything inside of me is now obligated to him or her. And hell, yes, I'm going to be all the father I want to be! As far as I'm concerned, there's no questions or doubts as to what has to be done now. We're getting married."

Her mouth fell open and with a hand to her throat, she stumbled back from him. "M-m-married?" she stuttered.

He breathed deeply as he tried to gather himself together. "That's what I said."

Dazed, her head jerked back and forth. "You don't want to get married!"

Something stronger than himself was suddenly pushing at him, putting words on his tongue and pushing them past his lips before his mind could access any of them. "What you and I want has nothing to do with it. We have a child to think of now. And we're going to do our duty."

For a moment he feared she was going to burst into tears, but then a chilling look of disgust filled her eyes, shocking him with its intensity. What did she have to be disappointed about? He was stepping up to the plate, being a man about this whole thing.

"Duty? That's what you think this is all about?" She made a choking noise, then whirled away from him. "I'm sorry, Quint. This is all wrong. I can't marry you!"

"Maura!"

Quint didn't have the chance to say more. She raced past him and out of the room.

Dazed, Quint continued to stand in the middle of the room as he tried to figure out how one minute he'd gone from expecting to have a simple visit with his grandfather, to maybe kissing a woman he'd missed, to hearing he was going to become a father. It was more than a normal man could absorb in one night.

Tossing his hat on the table, he raked a hand through his hair, then stalked out of the room.

Down the hallway, to his right, he found the door to Maura's bedroom shut and locked. He rapped the back of his hand against the dark wood.

"Maura," he said firmly. "Let me in. We have to talk about this."

There was a long pause, then eventually, through the barrier of the door, she said in a choked voice, "We don't *have* to do anything. I've already given you my answer, Quint. No! I won't marry you."

"Why?"

After a moment, she sputtered back at him, "Because you're not husband material."

Closing his eyes, he pinched the bridge of his nose, while wondering where he'd gone wrong in all of this. And why was he making such an issue out of getting married? Truth be known, he'd never held much passion for the idea. Being married meant commitment, sacrifice, sharing his life on a daily basis. He couldn't imagine himself in that role. And yet something was driving him, telling him that nothing would ever be right unless Maura became his wife. It didn't make sense.

Dear God, was he losing his mind, or was that stone in his chest finally breaking apart, allowing him to want and feel and love? No. Not that last part, he thought. Love wasn't making him act like an idiot. It was the simple task of trying to deal with a woman that was tearing up his common sense.

"If that's what you thought, then why did you go to bed with me in the first place?" he wanted to know.

"For the same reason you climbed between the sheets with me!" she muttered back at him. "I like having sex!"

For one second, Quint considered kicking the door in, but stopped himself short. His grandfather would be furious with him and clearly Maura wasn't thinking too kindly of him at the moment. Losing his temper wasn't going to fix anything.

Right now he wasn't sure anything could be fixed.

"We'll talk about this later, Maura," he told her. "When you're thinking straight."

"An arrow couldn't be as straight as my thinking is right now," she countered flatly.

Instead of him rattling the door handle or shouting a reply, Maura heard his boots echoing down the hallway, then the slam of a door. Moments later, she heard his truck fire, and the beam of his headlights swept across the bedroom window before finally disappearing into the night.

His leaving relieved her and yet she felt so flat, so cold and full of pain that all she could do was fall across the bed and burst into racking sobs.

Obligation! Duty! He'd demanded she become his wife. He'd not even had the decency to propose to her, to gently give her a choice in the matter!

*What did you expect, Maura? The man has never breathed the word* love *to you in any shape, form or fashion. The only connection he has to you is the child growing in your belly. Get your head out of the clouds and get used to it.*

The voice inside her head stiffened her spine somewhat and she rose to a sitting position and carefully wiped her eyes with the back of her hand.

For a few minutes, the existence of the baby had marred her common sense, she realized. Momentarily, she'd let herself believe that Quint considered her more than a bed partner and she'd expected him to treat her as a man with his soul mate.

Oh, God, how could she have allowed herself to get so off course? Quint was viewing this whole thing from a practical point. And she—well, she'd behaved like a lovesick teenager who'd just realized her boyfriend was out for one thing and one thing only.

It was mortifying and she wasn't going to let it happen again. She'd already had one husband who hadn't loved her. She wasn't about to make the same mistake over again. The next time she talked to Quint, she would be cool, calm and collected. And she was going to tell him in a quiet, unwavering manner, that under no circumstances would she ever become his wife.

No matter what.

# Chapter Nine

A little more than two weeks later, Maura sat with her mother on the couch in the Donovan family room. Once given the go-ahead, Bridget had wasted no time in spreading the news about Maura's pregnancy and for the past few days, each member of her family had, in their own way, offered her advice on the matter. Whether she'd asked for it or not.

In spite of Quint's continuing demands for her to marry him, Maura had persistently refused and all the Donovans believed she was making a mistake. Which only made her feel even more miserable about the whole predicament. As for Quint's family, Abe was clearly disappointed in her, but his mother, Frankie, had yet to say anything. Maura figured the woman felt as though she had no right to give advice on family matters. Not after she'd made some dicey choices of her own.

"Frankly, I don't understand you, Maura," Fiona said as she placed her teacup and saucer on the low table in front of them. "Quint is a respectable man. He's young and good-looking. And obviously you like him or you wouldn't be having his baby. Why don't you want to be his wife?"

The stubborn purse to Maura's lips broke as she let out a heavy sigh. "Mother, of all people, you shouldn't have to ask. You know what I went through with Gil. The humiliation, the dejection."

Her brows arched, the regal-looking woman leaned back against the couch. "What has Gil got to do with this? Surely you're not still carrying feelings for that hypocrite."

Rising from the couch, Maura walked over to the paned windows overlooking a view of the mountains. Compared to Quint's little house, the Donovan home was a lavish mansion and yet she'd felt completely comfortable there. Because he'd made the place special, she realized. He made everything special.

"Any feelings I had for Gil died a long time ago." Anguish twisted inside her chest and she closed her eyes as she prayed for the pain to go away. "I don't want to make another mistake, Mother. And Quint—he doesn't really want to be married. His desire to have us legally connected is all for the baby. Nothing else. I've had a marriage that wasn't based on a real love from both people and it didn't last. I don't want to be married to someone else who doesn't love me."

"And that bothers you."

With a muffled groan, Maura turned back to Fiona. "Of course it does!" she said, then swiping a helpless hand through her hair, she walked over to where she'd left her purse on the seat of a chair. "I'd better go, Mother. I told Bridget I'd meet her for lunch at the Blue Mesa. I'm going to have to hurry now to get there."

Quickly, Fiona rose from the couch and intercepted Maura before she could leave the room. "Darling," she said gently, "I understand what you want and need from Quint. But sometimes it's hard for a man to admit his feelings. Give him time."

The pain in Maura's chest dug deeper. "Quint doesn't love me. Time won't change that." Leaning forward, she pressed a kiss on her mother's cheek. "We'll talk about this later."

"Maura, please think about this carefully. If you care about Quint you should want to marry him. To try to make a life with him."

That was exactly why she didn't want to marry him, Maura thought. Because she loved him. Because deep down she considered his happiness far more important than hers. And he wouldn't be a happy man if he saddled himself to her out of obligation. And he'd never said anything about a life together—or even officially asked her out in public—before she found out she was pregnant.

"Goodbye, Mother. I'll call you soon."

On the drive leading off the Diamond D, she met Brady in his squad car, however when he waved at her and braked the vehicle to a stop, she just smiled at him and drove on. She'd already had one relative lecturing her this morning on the subject of Quint and no doubt over lunch Bridget would put her two cents in. Maura wasn't in the mood to deal with a third.

In Ruidoso, Maura was forced to park a block away from the Blue Mesa and walk back to the busy diner. Bridget was already there, sitting at one of the outside tables, which were all occupied by lunch-goers. She waved at Maura.

"I was lucky enough to get a table in the shade," she said as Maura pulled out a chair opposite her younger sister. "I hope you don't mind eating outside. The day is so lovely and I figured we could both use the fresh air."

"I'm just thrilled that I was able to smell food this morning without running to the bathroom and retching. But to be on the safe side, I only nibbled on dry toast for breakfast. So now I'm ravenous."

Chuckling, Bridget warned, "That will only get worse, dear sis."

Maura was shoving her handbag under the chair just as a waiter arrived at their table. After he'd taken their orders, Bridget asked, "Have you seen Quint lately?"

Even though she'd expected this from Bridget, she wasn't prepared for the bittersweet pain assaulting her senses. Not after she'd just gotten over the emotional exchange she'd had with her mother. Surely, she'd hurt enough for one day, she thought miserably.

"Two days ago. He came to Apache Wells. To see his grandfather, I assume."

Her pregnancy and refusal to marry him had thrown a cool wall between the two of them and Maura hated the distance between them. Every minute of the day she wished they could go back to being that man and woman making love at Chillicothe and the old hunting cabin. She missed being in his arms, missed the pleasure and joy of being close to him.

A frown puckered her sister's forehead. "Did you two talk?"

"Some. But nothing has changed, so don't bother asking," Maura said flatly.

Bridget simply retorted, "You're making a mistake, Maura."

Crossing her legs, Maura focused her gaze on the far distant peak of Sierra Blanca. The early autumn snows had yet to fall, but soon the white cap would appear. By then Maura's waist would be thick with Quint's child. The idea filled her with love, yet at the same time she felt totally lost. Where would her home be when the baby arrived? Would Quint still be interested in her and the child or would that end, too?

"I've made plenty of mistakes before," she said with wry sarcasm. "Why should I change now?"

"Maura! If a man like Quint wanted to marry me, do you know what I'd do? I'd jump at the chance!"

"Not if he didn't love you."

Bridget was clearly disgusted. "You clearly care for him. Doesn't that count? Doesn't that mean you want to be in his house, his bed?"

It did. But could Maura live with the idea that she was there only because of their child? Up until she'd met Quint, she'd always carefully weighed the decisions she'd made in her life. Even marrying Gil—though they'd only dated a few months—had been a thought-out process; at least, she'd believed she'd considered the serious step carefully, and by the time she'd walked down the aisle with him, she'd been twenty-nine years old. A mature woman. Not a teenager incapable of making important decisions. And yet with all her careful planning, she'd wound up getting her heart broken. Why in the world did her family expect her to jump into marriage now, without thinking, and to a man who didn't love her? A man who'd said he didn't believe in romance and never wanted to talk about feelings?

"Please, Bridget. I don't want to argue about this now.

That's all I've heard from Mother this morning and now you. I—"

Bridget threw up a both hands to ward off the rest of Maura's tirade. "Okay, sissy. I hear you loud and clear. We'll talk about something else."

Thankfully, Bridget kept her word and Maura managed to eat her lunch while the two of them discussed happenings at the hospital and the Donovan ranch.

Later, when the waiter questioned them about having dessert, Maura impulsively ordered a rich frosted brownie and decaffeinated coffee, then excused herself to find the bathroom.

As Maura rose to her feet, Bridget joked another warning, "That will get worse, too."

Maura arched a wry brow at her sister. "Is there anything that gets better with pregnancy?"

"Sure. Holding your little baby in your arms."

Maura smiled at her. "Thank you for reminding me, sis. And don't eat my brownie if it gets back to the table before I do."

Inside the restaurant, she made her way through the busy tables until she reached an annex where the ladies' room was located. Even that small space was filled to capacity, forcing her to wait in line until a stall was vacated.

Finally her turn came and she was still behind the locked cubicle, zipping her trousers, when she caught the sound of two women talking in hushed tones. Normally, Maura didn't take notice of that sort of thing. She didn't have the time or the appetite for gossip. But the words *pregnant* and *ranch* had caught her attention, causing her to purposely pause to catch more.

"—was the first time I saw her in ages. She looks gorgeous."

"Yeah. But divorced and pregnant. How would you like to have those problems on your plate?" the other woman responded.

Running water sounded, then the rip of paper towels. Above the noise, the first woman said, "I've been hearing lots of talk. You know she's been staying out at that old man's ranch."

"Yeah. Abe Cantrell," the second woman said, supplying the name. "Eccentric, I hear, but loaded to the gills with money. Guess he decided to buy himself some female attention."

"Well, I understand that some women are turned on by older men, but—" Woman One made a shuddering noise. "Having his baby. That's creepy."

Maura's fingers flew to her mouth. People were thinking she was pregnant with Abe's child? Oh, God, it couldn't be true! But it was! She was hearing it with her own ears.

"I'm just amazed that the old man is still that virile. He has to be in his eighties!" Woman Number Two exclaimed in a scandalous whisper, "And I sure can't figure the woman. She has plenty of her own money. Why would she be after his?"

"Who said she was?" Woman Number One giggled. "Maybe she's in it for the sex."

More laughter erupted before the two women finally shuffled out of the facility. By then Maura felt totally ill and though she wanted to race after the two women and confront them, she didn't. Other than humiliating herself, what good would it do? Assumptions about her and Abe had probably already spread over the county.

Stumbling to the lavatory, she splashed her face with cold water, then went out to rejoin Bridget.

As the two women finished their meal, Maura didn't mention the incident in the ladies' room. No doubt her family would hear the gossip soon enough and talking about it wouldn't ease Maura's guilt at marring the Donovan good name.

Later that afternoon, Quint was gritting his teeth, struggling to hold on to his temper, but Abe was pushing him to the breaking point.

He didn't know what in hell Abe was trying to do to him. Didn't he realize that his grandson had more serious things on his mind than reopening the Golden Spur? For the past week, his grandfather had continued to call and pester Quint about that damned old gold mine and, sick of arguing over the phone, Quint had decided to drive to Apache Wells and settle the matter once and for all. But as soon as he'd stepped through the door, Abe had dismissed the mine project and started pounding on him about Maura.

"Maura doesn't want to be my wife, Gramps! How many times do I have to tell you that?" Quint barked at his grandfather.

"She's gonna have your baby."

"Damn it all, don't you think I know that?" Quint muttered, then jumped up from the armchair he was in, left the living room and stalked to the kitchen.

Abe marched after him. "What are you gonna do about it?" the old man demanded. "Wait around until some other man grabs her? Some man that'll love her and make her happy?"

Quint jerked a beer from the bottom shelf, then turned to his grandfather as he twisted off the cap. "What am I supposed to do? Beg?"

Quint had never seen his grandfather look so furious. In fact, this was the first time he'd ever see the man truly angry with him. Sure, they often bantered in a sarcastic way, but they both understood it was done with underlying love. Abe's wasn't playing now and Quint was shaken by the change in him.

"Beg! That's not what Maura wants! And if you had half the sense I thought you had, you wouldn't have to be told what to do. You'd grab her—make her swoon, make her happy to be at your side!"

Quint was staring at his grandfather, wondering how he could possibly defend himself against that argument, when both men heard the bang of the screen door at the front of the house.

Momentarily stunned by the interruption, both turned to see Maura wearily entering the kitchen. She took one look at the two men, burst into tears and ran straight to Abe's arms.

"Here, here now, honey! What's all of this about?" he asked gently.

Hurt that she would run to Abe before coming to him, Quint stood to one side and wondered why he didn't have the right touch, the special words to bring her back to his arms. He'd never cared about that before, but somehow with Maura he hated that she'd gone to another man—even his grandfather—when she was troubled.

Pushing herself away from Abe's bony chest, she tried to dry her eyes. "Oh, Abe, people are talking! They think that you— That I'm having your baby!"

"Hellfire!" Quint barked with outrage.

A moment of silence passed before Abe finally slapped his knee and let out a loud whoop of laughter. "Well, I'll be damned. Me. Siring a baby. I didn't know I still had it in me!"

"Damn it, Gramps, this isn't funny!" Quint growled at him.

Folding his arms across his chest, Abe drew back his shoulders and grinned like a cat with a saucer of cream. "I sorta like it myself."

"Oh, Abe, it's terrible," Maura wailed. "They think I'm after your money or worse."

He swatted a dismissive hand through the air. "I know the truth. Who cares about a bunch of gossipin' tongues anyway."

"I do."

Maura and Quint spoke at the same time, causing Abe to level a long, measured look at the both of them.

"If that's the way you two feel then there's an easy way to put a stop to all the chin-waggin'. Get married."

Maura looked at Quint and felt something inside her snap with relief. She'd been resisting because she'd not wanted another one-sided marriage where she'd done all the loving. But to live with this man, under any circumstances, would be better than being alone, aching for the sound of his voice, the touch of his hand. And maybe someday he might actually grow to love her. She had to take that chance. She'd protect herself as best she could, holding back on admitting her feelings until she knew how he felt. Otherwise, she had no chance with him at all.

"Maura?" Quint gently questioned.

"I—" She licked her lips, then closed the last few steps between them. "Maybe it would be the best thing to do— for the baby."

A long breath eased from Quint and then he reached for

her. As he folded her into his arms, he said, "We'll be married as soon as possible."

Across the room, Abe smiled to himself and slipped out the door.

Fiona asked for a month to get the wedding organized, but instead Quint gave his future mother-in-law two weeks to prepare the church, ceremony and reception. The Donovan women worked overtime and when the day for the wedding finally rolled around, Our Lady of Guadalupe, the small church in Hondo Valley, was filled with flowers and music, flickering candlelight, family and well-wishers.

As the couple left the church beneath a rain of rice, the sky was sunny, the air crisp with the first nip of early fall. On the ride to the Donovan ranch, Quint could hardly take his eyes off Maura. He'd always heard the old saying that all brides were beautiful, but he couldn't imagine any woman looking more beautiful than Maura did today.

Her dress was creamy lace that framed her bosom with a heart-shaped V while the hem ended just below her knees. At the back of her head, her red hair was pinned in an elaborate twist and entwined with some sort of tiny, ivory-colored flowers that smelled sweet and alluring. Emeralds glistened in her ears and around her neck, yet the plain gold band on her left hand seemed far richer than any jewels Quint had ever seen. She was now Mrs. Quint Cantrell. A reality that was both heady and scary to Quint.

During the uncertain weeks after she'd told him about the pregnancy and up until today, they'd not made love. Not that Quint hadn't wanted to. Especially after she'd finally agreed to become his wife. These past days, every cell in him had been aching to be intimate with her again. But both of their schedules had been worse than hectic and the opportunity to be alone with her had never presented itself.

Now as he sat next to her in the back of the luxurious limousine that her family had provided, he could hardly keep his mind on anything else. And he wondered if, once they were on their honeymoon, she would be the same giving woman he'd made love to at the hunting cabin.

Her fight against this marriage had confused him and left him feeling very uncertain about their relationship, about her and even himself. Obviously she didn't love him. And he didn't expect that. Yet her reluctance to be his wife had stung him in a way he didn't want to think about. Especially not today, during this momentous time in their lives.

"I thought the ceremony was beautiful," he commented.

Smiling faintly, she glanced at him. "So did I. And I'm so glad your sister and brothers were able to fly in from Texas and attend. And that your brothers agreed to be your grooms."

Abe had been his best man and this morning as they'd prepared to head for the church, Quint had been shocked to see his grandfather all duded up in a dark Western suit, a bolo tie pushed tight against the collar of his starched white shirt. The old man had looked distinguished indeed and Quint couldn't help but wonder how Abe must have looked to his Grandmother Jenna all those years ago, when in the prime of their lives, they'd stood at the altar together.

Reaching for Maura's hand, he said gently, "I'm just very grateful that your family has accepted me like they have. With the baby and all—I wasn't sure what they were going to think of me."

Her lashes swept demurely against her cheeks. "Oh, Quint, they know this wasn't a case of you taking advantage of an innocent young woman. We're both—" She paused, her fingers instinctively tightening around his. "Responsible adults."

Yes. Responsible. That's why he'd wanted this marriage. To do the proper and responsible thing. So why didn't that rationale feel right whenever it was spoken out loud?

Shoving that troubling thought away, he changed to a more pleasant subject. "I hope you're happy about going to Hawaii for our honeymoon. I know it's a typical spot for newlyweds, but I thought—"

"I've never been to the Hawaiian Islands, Quint. I'm very pleased about going."

"Are you?"

Taken aback by his question, she turned toward him. "You don't sound as though you believe me. Why?"

He shrugged. "To be honest, I wasn't sure you'd even want to have a honeymoon or be in my bed again."

A pained look crossed her beautiful face and then with a muffled groan, she leaned close and rested her palm against the side of his cheek. Her touch was like a piece of sunshine after a hard, cold winter.

She whispered, "Just because I was against us getting married doesn't mean I want the relationship we had to end."

Relief poured through him and with a needy groan, he pulled her into his arms and didn't stop kissing her until they reached the Donovan house.

The honeymoon turned out to be far more lovely than Maura imagined it could be. For two long weeks they enjoyed the tropical climate, the beautiful beaches and each other. Quint couldn't seem to keep his hands off her and Maura had been completely surprised at just how he seemed to enjoy the tropical paradise and her.

But now that they were back on the Golden Spur and a month had passed, the memories of their honeymoon seemed almost surreal to Maura. As soon as they returned from Hawaii, Quint got back to the huge task of building the Spur into a profitable ranch and as each day went by, his attention seemed to grow more and more consumed with work, while Maura was left to keep herself occupied.

After Maura and Quint had married, Abe had quickly insisted that he no longer needed a nurse. His dizzy spells appeared to be a thing of the past and if he did come down with one, he assured them that Jim would be around to see after him.

Maura was glad Abe's health was well enough for him to do without her. She loved him as she had loved her own grandfather and wanted him to be able to actively enjoy his horses and ranch. But she missed being needed by the old man, missed the quiet evenings they'd spent simply talking about nothing in particular. Without any words, she'd understood that Abe liked her, even loved her. With Quint she couldn't quite discern what was going on behind his blue eyes, what was in his heart whenever he touched her. He would come home late and tired, and after a quick supper, generally just wanted to rest, not talk.

With Quint throwing his all into the ranch, Maura got busy creating a nursery in the spare bedroom. The task was a pure joy and she spent hours decorating the walls and windows, filling it with furniture, toys and baby necessities. But once the nursery was completed, she once again found herself puttering around the house, hunting anything to do to keep her mind occupied and off the uncertain bonds of her marriage.

Then one day when Maura was having lunch with Bridget, her sister offered her a light-duty nursing job at her private clinic. Maura was thrilled with the idea and that same evening when Quint returned to the house, she couldn't wait to tell him about her new job offer.

"You want to go to work?" he asked with surprise as the two of them sat down to dinner. "But why? There's no need for you to work."

"There's no need for you to work, either," she parried.

He grimaced as he plopped sour cream on a baked potato. "A man has to have a purpose."

"So does a woman," she argued. "And I'm not the aimless sort, Quint."

"You do all the bookkeeping for the ranch," he pointed out. "That's meaningful."

"At most, that takes me a couple of hours a week. I can't just sit around for the rest of the time. And in my condition, I can't help you with strenuous ranching chores. Nursing is my profession and Bridget needs me to cover another nurse who is taking some time off. And it's just for the next three months or so."

Looking up from his plate, his blue eyes searched her face. "But it's miles from town. You'll have a long drive every day getting to and from work."

She smiled at him. "I'm healthy and have plenty of energy. It'll be better for me to be occupied than sitting here bored."

Frowning, he picked up a steak knife and sliced through a strip of rare beef. "I thought you liked it here on the ranch," he said sullenly.

Seeing he misunderstood, she sighed. "I do like it, Quint. But—"

Glancing back up at her, he said, "Look, Maura, I know this house is old and needs some work here and there. That it's not nearly as nice as what you're accustomed to. But when we came back from Hawaii I offered for us to live at the Chaparral and you turned it down. Are you regretting that decision now?"

Vexed that he was getting so off course of the real issue, she shook her head. "Not at all. This is your home and—"

"It's not just my home. Now that we're married, it's yours, too," he interrupted with a bit of frustration. "If it's not good enough for you—"

She put down her fork and leaned back in her chair. "Quint, please slow down and quit being so defensive. This has nothing to do with the house. I need to have something to do. Are you against women working or something?"

"I'm not a caveman," he said sharply, then released a heavy breath. "I would never try to keep you from working, Maura. I just think—well, we hardly need the money. And we've not been married for very long. The baby is coming and I thought—"

He broke off and Maura waited patiently for him to continue, but instead he stubbornly returned his attention to his plate.

Maura said, "I'd like for you to finish, Quint. What were you thinking?"

He put down his fork and looked at her. Maura was immediately surprised to see a hint of color creeping up his neck and she wondered if it bothered him that much to express his real feelings to her. She hated to think so. Hated to think she was the one person in his life he couldn't talk to.

"This is going to sound stupid, especially since I—" He shook his head. "Forget that. What I'm trying to say is that

I thought you were a woman who would be satisfied with simpler things—a simpler life."

Not like Holly, who'd wanted more and more and not been satisfied until she'd ran off with another, Quint thought bitterly. Not like the women he'd later dated, who'd suggested he build a mansion or use his money to move to some island paradise.

"You're insulting me now, Quint," she said stiffly. "I don't want more or better things. You've seen the way I live. I was at your grandfather's home for a long while and his home is similar."

She was right. He was being insulting. Maura wasn't a spoiled rich girl. She wasn't even close to that. And there wasn't any reason for him to be putting up a fuss about her helping at her sister's clinic. He didn't know why he was behaving this way. Except that the moment she'd told him about the job, he'd viewed it as her drawing away from him, severing the few fragile threads holding them together.

Why he felt so unsure about their marriage, he didn't know. For the past six weeks since the wedding, she'd been like an adoring little kitten in his arms. When he asked her to make love, she never turned away. And yet he couldn't help feeling as though a part of her was vacant, as though that magical thing that he'd first felt between them had slowly and surely evaporated.

"I'm sorry, Maura. I wasn't thinking how it must be with you here most of the day by yourself—with little to do now that you've got the nursery and house in hand. If you want to work at Bridget's clinic, then go for it. You hardly need my permission anyway."

She got up from the table and retrieved a pitcher of iced water from the cabinet. As she refilled their glasses, she said, "No. Just like you don't need my permission when-

ever you leave the house in the mornings and return home
long after dark."

Her voice wasn't exactly cool or sharp, yet he felt cut
to the bone just the same. And he wondered sickly if this
was already the beginning of the end.

*What did you expect, you fool? She only agreed to
marry you because of the gossip and the baby. She's not
here because she wants to be your wife, to live in the same
house, share her life with you. And she's definitely not here
because she loves you. So forget it. You can play at being
man and wife, but it won't ever be the real thing.*

The voice inside him made Quint want to curse aloud.
Hell, what did that maudlin, sarcastic part of him know,
anyway? He didn't want Maura to love him. He didn't want
to love her. All he wanted was for them to be happy. And a
person didn't have to have love to be happy. Love only made
things complicated and painful. Being together was enough.
It had to be. Because living with Maura was one thing, while
having her love appeared to be beyond his reach.

## Chapter Ten

A few days later, Maura was stripping a used sheet from an examining table when Bridget walked in the small room and took her sister by the arm.

"Okay," she declared in an authoritative voice. "That's enough for today. You've not sat down since lunch." She forced Maura into the nearest plastic chair positioned against the wall. "Before you started this job we agreed you'd have light duty."

Maura waved a dismissive hand at her. "I'm not over-tiring myself. I'm enjoying this."

Bridget rested a hip against the table as she leveled a stern gaze at Maura. "Maybe so. But I want you to go home for the remainder of the day."

Maura glanced at her watch. "It's only three o'clock and you still have several patients to see," she insisted.

"And you have a long drive to the Golden Spur."

"Bridget—"

"If you're going to argue with me, I'll just have to fire you. Besides, you should be happy to get home early and see that husband of yours."

Maura grimaced. These days it was an effort to see Quint at all. He rose and left the house well before daylight and didn't come home until long after dark. The only chance she had to spend much time with her husband was on Sundays when the two of them attended church services together, then shared dinner afterward. Yet even then he seemed distracted and restless, as though spending time exclusively with her bothered him in some way. She understood he was in the process of building a new ranch and she understood that for a while, the project was going to consume his time. But she'd been getting the feeling that he was using his ranch work to deliberately stay away from the house and her. Why, she didn't know. She could only assume that he found it a relief to stay away from her.

"Quint won't be home until bedtime."

"Oh? He has something pressing going on?"

A familiar ache of tears suddenly clogged Maura's throat and she swallowed hard. Being pregnant was making her overly emotional, she told herself. It had nothing to do with Quint's distant behavior.

"No…he—" She broke off and wiped a trembling hand over her face. "I don't know what's going on with him, Brita. He doesn't seem to want to be with me anymore. We sleep in the same bed and we even make love. But a part of him is somewhere else." She turned a miserable gaze on her sister. "I think he regrets marrying me, but he's going through the motions because of the baby." Dropping her head in her hand, she swallowed again as tears now threatened the back of her eyes. "Everything he's done is because of the baby."

"I don't believe that."

Maura sighed. "Well, you'd better start believing it. Your practical sister has jumped straight into another heartache. God, I can't believe I stepped out of one terrible marriage only to turn around and jump into another! What's the matter with me, Brita? Don't I have any sense where men are concerned? I should have stuck to my guns and refused to marry Quint. That would have been better for both of us. Now he's miserable and I'm miserable."

"Have you talked to him about this? Told him your concerns?" Bridget asked.

Maura stared at her. "Why no! How could I? He told me he doesn't believe in romance, that he will never fall in love and doesn't want anyone to love him. I can't put the pressure of my love on him now!"

Bridget was rolling her eyes when a light knock sounded on the door and a young nurse named Michelle stuck her head into the room.

"Sorry to interrupt, Dr. Donovan, but Mrs. Montgomery is in examining room two and working her blood pressure up to the boiling point."

Bridget grimaced. "Okay, Michelle. I'll be there shortly. But kindly remind the woman that she's not the only patient around here."

"Yes, ma'am."

The nurse disappeared and Maura was once again caught in her sister's censuring gaze.

"Maura, you sound ridiculous," she scolded lightly. "You sleep in the same bed with Quint. You're his wife. You'd have to be a robot not to love the man. Surely he knows that."

Maura gave her head a rueful shake. "No. I told him it was only for the sex."

Clearly astounded, her sister's mouth dropped open. "Oh, Maura! You didn't! Why?"

Wadding the dirty sheet into a tight ball, Maura left the chair to stuff the white piece of fabric into a plastic hamper. "Because I—" Whirling back to her sister, she said in an anguished rush, "Look, Bridget, Gil pretty much shattered my self-worth. What he did to me made me feel worse than a fool. He didn't love me. He was using me. For the past year, I was doing my best to get over all that. And slowly I was learning to believe in myself again. Then when Quint came along and showed interest in me, my self-confidence as a woman really started to bloom. I thought that maybe I was still attractive to men. I thought that maybe—" She broke off as the pain in her chest rose up in her throat and she was forced to look away.

"What else were you thinking, sis?" Bridget urged after Maura failed to go on.

"Oh, Brita, before I got pregnant Quint and I were growing close—I mean, more than physically close. And I was starting to believe that maybe he really cared about me. That he might even grow to love me. But then when I told him about the baby, everything seemed to change. He didn't ask me to marry him, he demanded it. He mentioned nothing about caring for me or wanting me in his life. He didn't seem to have any consideration of my wants or needs. He just kept talking about duty and obligation and I was so hurt that I was determined not to let him stomp the last bit of my pride to pieces. I lashed back at him and that's when I told him that I'd slept with him only for the sex."

Bridget groaned with despair. "What a mess! You can't let this go on, Maura. You've got to tell Quint how you really feel about him or nothing is going to get better."

Maura wasn't so sure it could ever get better. But oh, God, how she desperately wanted it to.

Her knees suddenly week, Maura leaned against a work counter lined with first-aid items and medical instruments. "I don't know, Brita. I just don't know. Marriage, the baby—it all seemed to put a cool wall between us. The word *love*...I'm afraid it would only complicate things even worse."

Grimacing, Bridget pushed away from the examining table and headed toward the door. With her hand paused on the doorknob, she said, "Well, I can't see how that could be. But I'm hardly an authority on men and love. This is your life and your happiness. You're the one who'll have to do something to try to fix things—or ultimately regret it."

Back on the Golden Spur, Quint and Jake were riding the creek's edge, heading home after a morning of work that had taken them several miles northeast of the ranch yard.

A few minutes ago, they'd skirted old Chillicothe, and seeing the place where he'd first made love to Maura, even from a distance, had left Quint feeling more than melancholy. That trip with her had been very special to him. That day, for the first time in years, he'd felt excited about living, about the future. About having someone to share it with.

Had he loved Maura even then? For the past few months, he'd been telling himself that everything he did was not for her or for him. It was for the baby. But that wasn't entirely true. He didn't hold Maura in his arms each night only because her body excited him. He didn't want her as his wife simply because she was the mother of his child. He loved her. He hadn't planned on it, was afraid to tell her about it. So what did that make him? The biggest sap in the world?

"What's the matter, Quint? You've been quiet all afternoon."

Jake's question caused Quint's head to swing around toward his longtime friend. "Nothing is wrong. I've just had a lot on my mind. The past few days Gramps has been giving me hell about reopening the mine. He's like a dog with a bone. I tell you, Jake, I wished the damned thing was anywhere but here on my ranch property."

"Well, you just said the key word, buddy. This is *your* property. You can do what you want. If you're against opening the mine again, then put your foot down and tell the old man to quit yammering about it."

Quint grimaced as he contemplated Jake's suggestion. Even though the majority of Cantrell property was a shared conglomerate of the family, Abe had signed papers turning the Golden Spur property solely over to Quint. Yet in Quint's mind, that technicality hardly mattered. Family was family. He didn't want to hurt his grandfather over a blasted hole in the mountain.

"Jake, this ranch is mine because of Gramps. If not for him, I…my father…none of us Cantrells would have anything. Besides," he added glumly, "it's not just Gramps and the mine that has me distracted. Maura is—"

"What? Not feeling good?"

Quint's gaze dropped to the saddle horn as he easily envisioned Maura as she'd looked last night in a thin nightgown that had clung to her body. Her pregnancy was beginning to show and each time he looked at the rounded bump of her belly, he wanted to pull her into his arms and tell her how much he loved her and the baby.

But each time he got close to expressing his feelings, a sick sort of fear rushed over him. His throat clamped shut and his palms turned clammy. Marriage—a marriage only he'd wanted—had changed everything, had erected an invisible barrier between them that he couldn't seem to tear down. Telling her that he loved her might make it even worse.

"Her health is fine," he finally muttered.

Jake let out a long sigh. "I'm sorry, Quint, but you sound about as happy as a man who's just been thrown in jail. Didn't I tell you not to marry the woman? You didn't have to do that to be a good father to the kid. Now you're all glum and moody and worrying if you're gonna lose her."

Quint's head jerked up. "Why do you say that? You think Maura is going to leave me? Does she act that unhappy to you, too?"

Jake cursed as he maneuvered his horse away from a patch of prickly pear. "Worry. That's all a man ever does when he loves a beautiful woman. First he frets about catching her. And then when he does get his hands on her, he worries himself silly wondering if he'll be able to keep her."

Quint hated to admit it, but his cynical friend was right. From the moment he'd kissed Maura at the altar, he'd known that their marriage was a bargain for the baby's sake, not something with a real foundation. How long could he expect it to last?

Once they reached the ranch yard and Quint began to unsaddle his mount, he was still asking himself that same question. But the answer wouldn't come.

When the cell phone in his pocket shrilled loudly, the distraction was somewhat of a relief. Until he saw it was his grandfather calling. For the old man to ring his cell phone, it had to be something important. Or at least, important to Abe.

"Hello, Gramps," he said as he held the phone with one hand and used the other to place a sweaty horse blanket over the top rail of a wooden fence. "Are you all right?"

"Hell, yes, I'm all right! I'm talking to you, ain't I?"

Quint breathed deeply and tried to hang on to his patience. "You normally ring the house phone."

"I've learned that doesn't do anything but waste time. You're never in the house and Maura ain't, either. Now that you've let her go to work," he added with undisguised sarcasm.

Quint led his dun-colored mount, Champ, over to a nearby stall and slipped the bridle from his mouth.

"I don't 'let' Maura do anything," Quint drawled. "She's a grown woman. She does what she wants to."

Abe snorted. "Have you forgot that she's pregnant?"

"You didn't appear to be worried about that when she was working for you," Quint countered.

There was a long pause and then Abe said, "I ain't callin' about Maura. I want you to get over here. I just got off the phone with the big shot of Red Bluff. He's given me some estimates and I want to go over them with you. And not over the damned phone, either."

His teeth grinding together, Quint locked the gate on the stall and started out of the barn. "You went behind my back and called the man?"

Insulted, Abe practically shouted, "Behind your back? It ain't like we haven't talked about this for months. I'm gettin' tired of you bein' so wishy-washy and sittin' on your—"

"All right!" Quint practically shouted. "I'm coming over there right now! We're going to get this mining thing settled once and for all. And this time, I mean it!"

Abe's reply to that was to slam the telephone receiver back on the hook.

Halfway across the ranch yard, Quint met Jake. "Feed Champ for me," Quint told him. "I've got to go to Apache Wells. Once you get the feeding done, you might as well call it a day. I won't be back before late."

Shaking his head, Jake gave him an affectionate slap on the shoulder. "Don't worry about things here, buddy. Just do what you have to do."

On the drive home, Maura wrestled with the idea of having a heart-to-heart talk with Quint tonight. Perhaps Bridget was right. If he understood how much she loved him, then he might view their whole marriage in a different way. If it would even draw him back to the way he'd been with her before she'd told him about the baby, then it would be worth the risk, she decided, as she parked her car at the side of their small ranch house.

She didn't how she was going to approach him or even find the nerve to confess her love, but she had to find the courage somewhere.

Inside the house, she put her things away, then went to the kitchen to see what she could find toward making a special meal for the evening ahead. Instead, she found a note Quint had left lying on the kitchen table, telling her that he'd gone to see his grandfather and not to expect him back for supper.

Terribly disappointed, Maura walked over to the wall of windows and tried not to cry as she stared out at the sea of cholla cacti and sage sweeping to the west. How many days, months, years had she sat at home alone, waiting for Gil to decide he wanted to spend time with her? She couldn't begin to count those lonely, unhappy days and nights. Now, after swearing to never let another man hurt her, she was back on the same path, waiting for a man, even though she clearly knew that man didn't love her.

Was she crazy or just one of those people who couldn't help but walk down a path of self-destruction?

Later that evening, just before dark settled over the ranch, Maura forced down a light meal then went to sit on the front porch. Cuddled in a thick sweater and sipping coffee from a thermal mug, she was suddenly surprised by the sound of a vehicle coming from the direction of the ranch yard. Had Jake or one of the building contractors stayed behind to work late?

Before she could rise to go look, she spotted Jake's pickup truck pulling through the ranch yard gate. Obviously the man had stayed behind to finish an important task and was just now heading home. A place, which Quint had told her, was a small piece of property near Fort Stanton.

Since Maura had come to live on the Golden Spur, she'd gotten to know Quint's best friend and ranch hand a bit better. But she doubted anyone, other than her husband, knew the man completely. Gradually, she'd discovered he was a man of contradictions. On the surface he seemed to take life and himself as a joke, yet there had been moments when Maura had seen him staring off in the distance, his thoughts obviously too deep for him to share.

Lowering her cup, she watched him carefully latch the gate behind him then climb back into his truck. Fully expecting him to turn onto the long dirt road leading away from the ranch, she was bemused to see him brake to a stop in front of the house.

As he walked across the small yard toward the porch, she noticed he was dressed in clean jeans and a starched white shirt. Clearly, he was headed somewhere other than home and had used the facilities in the barn to freshen up.

"Good evening, Jake," she greeted.

Lifting a black hat from his head, he held it politely at his side. "Evening, Maura. I saw you sitting out here and thought I'd stop by. See if you needed anything before I left for town."

"That was thoughtful of you. But I can't think of anything—except for my husband to come home," she added wistfully.

A benevolent smile curved the corners of his mouth. "I think he and his grandfather were going at it over something. I expect he'll be home shortly."

"I hope you're right," Maura said, trying her best to sound lighthearted, but failing miserably. She gestured toward a chair positioned a few feet away from her. "Would you like to sit and have a cup of coffee? The pot is still fresh."

He stepped onto the porch and eased onto the edge of a bent willow chair. "I'll sit for a moment. But I'll have to pass on the coffee. I've got to get to Ruidoso in about forty minutes."

"Looks like you're on your way to a special outing," she observed.

His chuckle was a bit self-conscious and Maura smiled to herself. Apparently, Jake was planning to enjoy a bit of female companionship tonight and she was glad. Like Quint, the man worked far too hard and, as far as she knew, did very little socializing.

"Just a little date with Rita Baxter."

Maura tried to hide her disapproval, but it must have shown on her face because his features crinkled into a comical frown.

"Looks like you don't think too highly of Rita," he said.

Maura made an issue of straightening her sweater as she tried to think of the best way to reply. Jake was such a devoted friend that she hated to hurt his feelings. But Rita was not the right woman for him. True, she was from a well-to-do family and ran a popular souvenir shop in Ruidoso, but she used men for her own benefit.

"Well, have you known her long?"

"Oh. I wouldn't say that I could write her life history. But I've been acquainted with the woman for a while. Ever since she started showing up at the Finish Line—you know, the nightclub out by the track. Before that—well, I never traveled in that rich of a social circle."

She slanted him a droll look. "Jake, you can't get much richer than Quint and you've been traveling in his circle for years."

He batted a dismissive hand through the air. "Shoot, that's different, Maura. Quint might be rich, but he don't act it. Most folks wouldn't know he and his family own half the county unless you told them. But Rita—well, I think she likes flaunting what she has."

Maura let out a breath of relief. "So you know that—"

"She's a man-eater?" he finished with a sly grin.

A blush stung Maura's face. "Well, I wasn't going to describe her quite that way. But since you brought it up, yes. She's out for herself. And I happen to think you could do a whole lot better than Rita Baxter."

He surprised her with a low chuckle. "Thanks, Maura. But you don't have to warn me about her. I know what she is."

Confused now, Maura shook her head. "If you know, then why are you dating her?"

His grin was tinged with wry resignation. "Because I'm not nearly as lucky as Quint. I don't have a good woman like you to come home to every night. I have to settle for something far less."

Maura was so momentarily stunned by his remark she didn't know what to say. After Gil's infidelity, she'd believed she must be lacking, that a decent man would never give her a second thought. Now she could see how ridiculous that sort of thinking had been. She was a good woman. And she had lots to offer Quint and their marriage. If only he would open his heart and accept her love.

"That's nice of you, Jake. But take it from me, don't ever sell yourself short. And most of all, don't let Rita get her hooks into you."

Rising to his feet, Jake plopped his hat on his head. "No chance in that happening, Maura. I've got my eyes wide-open." He stepped off the porch, then gave her a little wave as he headed back out to his truck.

As Maura watched the man drive away, she decided that she finally had her eyes wide-open, too. Her marriage might not have started under the best conditions, but she wanted it to succeed. She wanted it to be real and lasting. And somehow, someway, she was going to make that clear to her husband.

Much later that night, long after Maura had gone to bed, she heard Quint when he walked into the bedroom and, without bothering to turn on the light, began to undress.

Maura glanced at the digital clock near the head of the bed: 12:10 a.m.

"Is Abe okay?" she murmured drowsily as he climbed into bed.

"He's fine," he said curtly. "We had things to discuss."

She scooted closer to his warm body and rested her hand upon his arm. "Oh. What sort of things?"

He lay on his back and though it was dark inside the room, Maura instinctively knew he was staring up at the ceiling. And then his hand reached across and briefly touched her shoulder.

"I'll tell you about it later," he said tiredly. "Right now it's late. We'd better get to sleep."

"Yes. Good night," she muttered stiffly.

Rolling to her side, she squeezed her eyes shut while she tried to push away the hollow disappointment filling her heart. Everything inside her wanted to reach for him, to beg him to make love to her, but he wasn't giving her any initiative and in her emotional condition, she could hardly handle a rejection.

After several long moments had passed and she'd heard his breathing slow, he said, "I'm sorry I wasn't here for supper."

She swallowed as tears threatened to overtake her. There was so much she wanted, needed to say to him. But the timing was rotten and the risk too great, so she swallowed away the words of love and kept it simple. "That's okay, Quint. I understand you have other things to take care of."

"Do you really?"

The doubt in his voice confused and angered her, making her reply come out sharper than she intended. "I like to think I'm an understanding woman, Quint."

"You sure sound like it."

A heavy sigh rushed past her lips. "I missed you, Quint. That's all."

"Look, Maura, you ought to know I'm not trying to ignore you. Right now I'm carrying a hell of a load. I just can't carry any more."

In other words, she and the coming baby had only added to his mountain of responsibilities. She wanted to scream at him, to ask him why he'd demanded that they marry in the first place. But getting into a shouting match in the middle of the night wouldn't solve anything.

"And whose fault is that, Quint? Mine?"

After several tense moments, his head turned on the pillow and she could feel his gaze studying her in the semidarkness.

"Don't say that, Maura."

She bit down on her lip as pain stabbed the middle of her chest. "You can only spread yourself so thin, Quint. Maybe it's time you decided what's most important to you."

His sigh was as heavy as a rock falling into a pool of water. "Yeah. I guess you're right."

The next morning Jake called Quint to say his mother was having some sort of problem with the pump on her water well and he'd be late getting to the ranch. Since he couldn't start much of a project without his right-hand man, Quint used the time to drive down to Ruidoso Grain and Tack and pick up several things he'd been needing, including several pairs of horseshoes and the nails to go with them.

Throughout the drive, he tried to focus his attention on the radio and the local market report, but his mind wasn't having any of it. All he could think about was Maura and the lovely way she'd looked this morning when he'd left her sleeping in their bed.

He didn't know what had made him snap at her last night. He couldn't use exhaustion as an excuse, since he was more often than not dog tired when he got home to the house each night. But something about the disappointment in her voice had stabbed him where it hurt the most. He'd not expected that from Maura. Holly, yes. But not Maura. He'd always thought of his wife as a truly unselfish woman, one who would never make demands on him.

*She wasn't making demands, Quint. She was trying to tell you that she's unhappy. And it's time for you to change all of that.*

But how, Quint wondered. How could he expect to keep a special woman like Maura happy?

*"Maybe it's time you decided what's most important to you."*

What had she meant by that? he asked himself. That he give up the things he loved to devote his time completely to her? Or was she trying to say she simply wanted to be included in the things he loved? Oh, God, he wished he knew. He needed to make time to talk to her. To find out what was going on. They couldn't keep going like this once the baby was here.

A few minutes later, Quint picked up the items he needed from the feed store, then at the last minute decided to grab a cup of coffee and a pastry at the Blue Mesa before he made the long drive back to the ranch.

At an outside table, he was draining the last of his cup, when he heard someone call his name from behind. Glancing over his shoulder, he was more than stunned to see Vince Johnson approaching him.

Holly's parents had been gone from Lincoln County for at least five or six years and Quint hadn't spoken to any of the family since the breakup seven years ago. The odds of running in to Vince like this had to be impossible. And especially on a day when he wasn't in the humor for raking up the past. In fact, he wasn't much in the humor for anything. Damn it all, he was having the worst of luck this morning and once he got back to the ranch, he was going to let Jake know he was half the cause of it!

"Quint! I thought that was you!"

Smiling, the older man extended his hand and in spite of being weighed down with frustration, Quint rose politely to his feet and shook it. "Hello, Vince. This is a surprise. I heard you'd moved to Nevada."

The tall, graying man nodded. "That's right, we call Beatty home now. We're just here for a little visit with the wife's cousins. They still live over at Alto." With another wide smile, he patted Quint's shoulder. "How have you been? Still ranching?"

"I'm okay. We lost Dad a couple of years ago. So I'm seeing after the ranches now."

The other man's expression turned rueful. "Yeah. We heard about Lewis passing. I'm so sorry, Quint. He was a good man. Guess that's why he raised such a good son."

Quint glanced skeptically at him, then let out an awkward laugh. "I almost believe you mean that."

Vince Johnson stared straight at him. "Well, hell, yes, I mean it," he said with conviction. "Why wouldn't I?"

"After Holly—"

"Oh, my daughter," he interrupted with a shake of his head. "After she went to Denver I don't think I ever had the chance to tell you how sorry I was about her behavior."

"It wasn't your place to apologize," Quint assured him.

"Well, I just wanted you to know that her mother and I never approved of what she did to you. Damn it, we still don't approve of her behavior. But she's a grown woman and what's a parent to do? Tell her how to live her life?"

"I couldn't say, Vince. I don't have any children." *Yet*, he thought. But soon he would be a father and raising that child to be a decent, honest human being was going to be his first priority in life. That and Maura.

With a tight grimace, the older man glanced around as though to make sure no one close was listening, then settled his gaze back on Quint. "Let me tell you something, Quint, the Lord blessed you when he took Holly off your hands."

The Johnsons used to dote on their young daughter, so it more than surprised Quint to heart Vince talk about Holly in such a negative way.

"You think so?"

"Oh, hell, son, she's not turned out the way that we'd hoped. But then, I suppose me and Joyce made everything too easy for her. Now, she drinks too much and spends money like it's water. Her kids are monsters but what should we expect when they have no supervision? Not with their parents on the road all the time."

"I'm sorry to hear that," Quint said, and he meant it. All of a sudden, he realized that he held no ill wishes toward Holly. In fact, now that he was listening to Vince talk of his daughter, it struck him that he felt nothing except relief that he'd been dealt a far better hand. He now had a beautiful wife who was going to give him a child. Being bitter about the past held no place in his life anymore.

"It's a mystery to me why she had the kids in the first place," Vince went on. "Just to solidify her marriage is my guess. You see, Robert, her husband, was pretty much of a playboy when she married him. I guess she thought the kids would anchor him. Hell, if you ask me the two of them deserve each other."

"But the children don't deserve that," Quint replied.

Vince released a heavy breath. "No. You're right about that. Joyce and I are thinking of bringing them out to Beatty to live with us. We're a little old to be raising kids now, but something has to be done. Let's just hope we don't make the same mistakes with them as we did with Holly."

The faint smile on Quint's face said he wished the man luck. "We all live and learn, Vince."

"Yeah. Isn't that the truth," he said, then clearing his throat, he slapped Quint on the shoulder again. "It's been good to see you, Quint. Why, it was just the other day that Joyce was saying she wished you'd been our son-in-law instead of Robert. I told her you're too nice a young man to be wishing that sort of trouble on."

He chuckled as he finished his last remark, and for a split second Quint stared quizzically at the man before he, too, began laughing. Running into Vince Johnson this morning hadn't been a curse at all, he realized. It was an eye-opener. He'd not lost Holly because he'd done anything wrong. Or because he'd not been man enough to hold on to her. She'd left because of her own self-satisfying interests. And from the things Vince had said about her, it sounded as though she was still chasing around, trying to find something or someone to make her happy.

But Quint didn't have to wonder what made him happy. It was Maura. He'd been fortunate enough to find her, love her, make a baby with her. And somehow, someway, he was going to have to make her see just how important she and their coming baby had become to him.

The two men exchanged goodbyes and Quint walked away from the Blue Mesa, feeling as though he'd just shed a ton of garbage from his shoulders.

Later that afternoon, on the Golden Spur, while Jake and Quint were busy shoeing horses, the ring of Quint's cell phone interrupted their progress.

"You might want to ignore that," Jake joked. "It might be Abe again wanting you to go back over to Apache Wells."

"Not after last night," Quint told the other man. "He was so angry at me he could have spit nails. I figure it'll be a while before I hear from Gramps again."

Stepping back from the horse, Quint dug the phone from his pocket, while hoping the caller ID would be illuminating Maura's name. There had been a few times during her afternoon break at work she would call for a brief chat, but like Abe, after last night she was probably too angry with him to bother, he thought ruefully. All afternoon he'd been tempted to call her and apologize, to let her know he could hardly wait for her to get home. But he feared he'd interrupt her work at the worst possible moment. Besides that, he figured she deserved an apology in person. She deserved so much more than she'd been getting from him and he wanted to be standing face-to-face with her whenever he told her so.

Quickly turning the phone upright, Quint was suddenly jerked from his thoughts of Maura. The caller was Mac, his brother in Texas! What was he doing calling in the middle of the afternoon? First Vince Johnson this morning and now Mac this afternoon. This day was certainly turning out to be full of the unexpected, he thought drily.

"I gotta take this, Jake," he said to the other man, then quickly moved over to a quiet spot in the shade of the barn and flipped open the phone.

"Mac!" Quint greeted. "This is a surprise!"

The other man chuckled. "I have a little coffee break going on and thought I'd call and see how my brother is doing. Do you have a minute?"

Quint glanced across the way to see Jake was still hard at work, fitting a shoe to the horse's hind hoof, but the animal was behaving nicely and Jake could handle the task without Quint's help.

"Sure. We're just doing a little farrier work this afternoon."

Mac chuckled again. "See, when you live in sandy south Texas, you don't have to worry about horseshoes," his brother teased.

"So Alexa tells me," Quint said wryly, then proceeded to ask him about his family.

After Mac had assured him that everyone was doing good, he said, "Actually, I was calling to see how you're doing, Quint. I'm worried about you."

Quint stiffened. "Don't tell me. Abe called and tried to enlist your aid in persuading me to reopen the Spur."

"As a matter of fact, he did call, but we didn't talk that much about the old mine," Mac admitted, then paused for a long moment. "He seems to think you're very unhappy. I told him he must be wrong. You're married to a sweet, beautiful woman and you're going to have a baby. You're getting your ranch shaped up and running—there's no reason for you to be unhappy. Is there?"

Quint let out a long, heavy breath. "Not at all. I'm sorry he bothered you with such an idea, Mac. He should have told you the real reason I'm upset—that's he's hounding me to death about reopening the mine. I told him last night that I flat-out oppose it. But Abe doesn't always hear the word *no*."

"Well, I'm not one to pry, Quint. I just promised the old man that I'd call, so I'm keeping my promise. I'm glad there's nothing wrong with you and Maura. You two seemed very happy at the wedding."

Had they? Their wedding day had passed in a haze for him, yet he remembered the sense of being happy, remembered thinking that having Maura as his wife felt right and good. And even through the honeymoon, he'd felt so contented to have her wrapped in his arms each night.

It wasn't until they'd gotten home that reality had struck Quint like a bolt of lightning. He'd looked around at the ranch he'd worked so hard to build and it had dawned on him that none of it would mean anything without Maura.

And that had scared him. He'd never wanted to be that emotionally dependent on any woman. He'd not wanted his happiness to be wound up so deeply in another human being. But now it was and he couldn't hide from his feelings any longer.

"Mac, I—I'm not being entirely honest," he said with a sudden rush. "I am aggravated about dealing with the mine issue. But to tell you the truth, what I'm really miserable about is Maura and me."

"Why?"

"Because I've realized that I love her. Love her with all my heart."

Mac paused and when he spoke again, Quint could hear a smile in his voice.

"Yeah. I know the feeling. When you think about it, about her, you get kinda shaky and scared and angry all at once. All you can think about is how vulnerable she makes you feel and how awful life would be without her."

Quint let out a breath of relief. "Oh, hell, Mac, will it always be this way?"

"It won't if you'll quit running scared and tell Maura how you really feel," he said, then added, "And if that's not enough to convince you, just think about how much our mother lost, Quint, because she hid her fears from the people she loved the most. You don't want that to happen to you."

Quint stared across the ranch yard to the house. There were still a few hours to go before Maura returned from work. Tonight after she got home, he wasn't going to hold back. Win, lose or draw, he was going to let her know how very much he loved her. But would she believe him? God, he could only hope. "No. Mother—all of us—lost too much," Quint agreed.

"And by the way," Mac went on, "I realize your grandfather can be a handful to deal with. But he has your interests at heart. And you need to remember that he made his fortune by taking chances. It might not hurt for you to take a chance on him."

"And go along with that cockamamie plan of his to hunt for gold?" Quint countered with disbelief. "Mac, I thought you were a practical man."

He laughed with genuine amusement. "Ileana has changed me. Besides, Mom says that before Abe struck oil in Texas, people called him all sorts of a fool. But he stuck to his guns and proved them wrong. Maybe you ought to rethink your decision about reopening the mine, Quint. If it turned out to be a producer, it would be a nice legacy for the baby."

"I'll think about it, Mac. And—"

"Oops, sorry, brother. I gotta go," Mac interrupted abruptly. "I'm on duty and it's an emergency. Call me later."

Mac swiftly ended the call and Quint thoughtfully slipped the phone back into his pocket. He should have been furious with Abe for calling Mac and dragging him into his personal problems. But deep down, Quint couldn't be angry with his grandfather. Somehow Abe had realized that talking with his older brother was just the sort of thing Quint needed.

With sudden resolve, he walked back over to where Jake was finishing the last shoe on Ramrod.

"Don't worry about shoeing the other horse right now," Quint told him. "We'll work on him tomorrow. While there's still some daylight left, I'm going to drive out to the old mine and take a look around."

Jake looked at him with surprise. "The Spur? You need me to come along?"

"No. Go ahead and ride the filly. We need to get her ready for pasture work. I'll be back in a little while," Quint told him.

Thankfully, Bridget's clinic was filled with patients throughout the day and that kept Maura very busy until closing time. While she'd taken blood pressures and temperatures and registered information in charts, she'd tried to focus entirely on her work and not on her husband's cool behavior toward her.

But that was easier said than done and in spite of listening to a drone of aches and pains from the patients, Maura longed to lay her head down in some quiet place and weep her eyes out.

"Maura, wait a minute! You can't leave yet!"

Pausing at the door, Maura glanced over her shoulder to see Bridget hurrying toward her. She'd shed her lab coat and reading glasses and looked more like her little sister than the harried physician who hardly took a moment for herself.

"I peeked in your office to say goodbye for the day," Maura told her. "But you were on the phone."

Bridget grimaced. "Discussing treatment for the Hollister baby. I'm sending him to a cardiologist in Albuquerque."

Maura's hand settled protectively over her growing stomach. Every day, every night, she prayed to God that her child would be healthy.

"Is there hope that the little fella's heart can be fixed?" Maura asked.

Bridget pressed fingers to her furrowed brow. "There's always hope, Maura. And I think his chances to grow up and lead a normal life are good."

Maura sighed with relief. She was familiar with the

Hollister baby and his mother and she desperately wanted things to turn out good for them.

"I'm so glad," she said, then arched a questioning brow at her sister. "Did you stop me for some other reason?"

Bridget caught her by the arm and began leading her back to her office. "I most certainly did."

After ushering Maura into the small room and shutting the door behind them, she said, "We've not had a chance to say more than two words to each other all day. And I want to hear how things went with you and Quint last night. Did you have that talk with him, like I suggested?"

A heavy sigh slipped from Maura. "I didn't have the chance. When I got home Quint had gone to his grandfather's and didn't come home until after midnight. By the time I got up this morning, he'd already left the house."

"I see." She thoughtfully chewed her bottom lip. "Well, I've thought about this a lot since we talked yesterday and I think—" She leveled a troubled glance at Maura. "There's something I think I'd better tell you."

An uneasy chill rippled down Maura's spine. Was something wrong with someone in the family? With Abe? It wasn't like Bridget to be secretive. "Tell me what? Did Quint go to see Abe because his grandfather is ill? Is that why he didn't want to talk to me about the visit?"

Bridget's expression suddenly turned rueful. "No, no. It's nothing like that. It's nothing to do with anyone's health. Except maybe yours," she added bleakly.

Maura sank into the plush leather chair positioned in front of Bridget's desk. "What are you talking about?"

Facing her sister, Bridget rested a hip on the corner of the desk. "All right. A few days ago, during my lunch break, I drove down to the Blue Mesa."

Maura groaned. "Oh, God, Brita, don't tell me you heard more gossip about me and Abe!"

"I haven't heard a word about any of that. What I'm trying to tell you is that on my way back here to the clinic, I saw Quint."

"Quint? Here in town?" It wasn't often that her husband drove into Ruidoso. He wasn't the type to enjoy urban attractions. Even the small-town kind. And if the ranch needed supplies, Jake always drove in to collect them.

Bridget nodded. "I wasn't going to tell you. And it's probably nothing, but well, he was coming out of a lawyer's office. The one down on Sudderth. Phillips, Andrews and Phillips, I think."

Bridget might as well have thrown ice water in Maura's face. She was so shocked, all she could do was stare in stunned silence at her sister. Finally, she asked in a raw whisper, "Quint went to a lawyer? Did you talk to him?"

"No! I was in the car and I didn't stop or wave to him. Actually, I didn't want him to know that I'd seen him. I was concerned that—" She broke off with a frown. "Has he mentioned seeing a lawyer about anything?"

Maura's eyes widened as the pit of her stomach turned to lead weight. "No! But then Quint doesn't do a lot of talking. I— Oh, God, Bridget! Maybe he's already decided he wants a divorce and wanted to discuss his rights to the baby?"

Bridget closed the short space between them and placed a steadying hand on Maura's shoulder. "Don't go jumping to conclusions like that. I happen to think that Quint loves you. But he might be confused about your feelings and—"

Maura instantly shot to her feet. "I've got to get home, Brita! I've got to talk to him. Now! As soon as I get there!"

But as Maura headed her truck toward the Golden Spur, she couldn't help but wonder if she'd waited too long.

## Chapter Eleven

Dust fogged in the wake of Maura's truck as she sped down the last mile to the ranch house, then braked to a stop next to Quint's vehicle.

Inside the house, she called his name, then after finding the rooms empty, she didn't bother changing from her green scrubs before she hurried to the barn.

Halfway there, she spotted Jake riding a painted filly in the training pen, so she turned on her heel and walked in his direction.

"You looking for Quint?" he called out to her from atop the nervous horse.

"Yes. Is he at the barn?"

"No. He drove the old four-wheel drive out to the mine."

As Maura reached the board fence of the training pen, she frowned with confusion. "The mine? Whatever for?"

Jake shrugged. "I don't know. He got a phone call from somebody. He didn't say who and then he just took off. Frankly, Maura, I'm worried about him. Quint's made of iron, but a man can just take so much. And Abe—"

"Yes, yes, I know, Jake! I'm going out there now to find Quint. Has he been gone long?"

Jake glanced at his watch. "A couple of hours, at least. Do you want me to go with you?"

Maura shook her head. "No thanks, I can find it."

"Well, if you have any trouble, you have my cell number," he reminded her.

Maura thanked him again, then hurried back to the house. There she quickly threw on blue jeans, a heavy shirt and boots, then jumped into her truck and sped back down the graveled road. Five miles east, another road turned to the left and curved a snaky loop back into the mountains. Maura had never traveled the road, but Quint had told her it was a shortcut to Chillicothe. Since the mine was near the old town, it would be the best route for her to take.

During the rough ride, Maura clung to the steering wheel, while her mind whirled with Jake's words.

*Quint's made of iron, but a man can just take so much.*

Why hadn't Maura thought of that sooner? For the past year and a half Quint had put in long, endless hours building this ranch. And all during that time he'd been seeing after his grandfather's health, along with the old man's demands. And still recovering from the shock of learning his mother had another family, his sister's pregnancy and then marriage to a Texas Ranger. Then he'd gotten entangled with Maura and suddenly he was faced with a wife and a coming baby. No doubt all of those things together had stretched Quint thin and pulled his emotions in all directions. Instead of her whining and worrying herself about him not giving her the right attention, she should have been busy trying to become a real partner for him, and showing how much his happiness meant to her. To love—really love—meant to give. Not take.

By the time she reached the mine, the sun was dipping toward the horizon, but there was still at least an hour of sunlight left.

The old ranch truck was parked a short distance from the entrance to the shaft, yet Quint was nowhere in sight. After parking her own vehicle, she climbed out and began to search and call his name.

"Quint?" she called. "Where are you?"

Her voice bounced off the mountain walls and echoed back to her, but Quint's voice didn't follow.

Deciding she was wasting time, she pulled out her cell phone and punched his number. It tried to ring once but the sound was erratic and then the connection was cut off completely. After three attempts with the same result, she realized the tower signal was too far away and reaching him by phone was impossible, so she slipped the phone back into her jeans pocket and began to search the narrow canyon that traveled a hundred yards or more east of the shaft entrance.

After several more minutes of searching with no sign of him, Maura began to worry that the only place left for Quint to be was inside the mine. Being underground would have certainly blocked off her cell phone signal to him.

But why would he have entered the dangerous cave? Especially after he'd warned her that it was unsafe? Was he so unhappy that he didn't care if he put his own life in jeopardy? Surely he would think about the baby!

For a moment she considered calling Jake. But she didn't want to alarm the man. Add to that, it would take him at least thirty minutes of hard driving to get out here, so she cast that notion aside and hurried to her truck for a flashlight.

At the mine entrance, she stuck her head just inside the dark interior and called out, "Quint? Are you in here? Please, answer!"

Maura waited for a reply, but all she could hear was a faint *drip, drip*. After a quick search with her light, she could see the source of the noise was coming from the ceiling of the tunnel. Small leaks of orange-and-yellow-tinted water were falling to the rock-strewn floor, creating gummy puddles of liquid minerals that eventually spilled over and made a slow trickle out the open doorway and down the side of the foothill.

After another loud yell out to her husband, Maura decided she had no choice but to go into the cave to search for him. Clearly he'd been gone far longer than what it would take a person to have a simple look over the outside area.

Drawing in a deep breath, Maura aimed the flashlight to the ground in front of her, then stepped inside the dank mine. The air was a tad warmer than outside and smelled of wet rocks and something indefinable like sulfur or some sort of metal. The sound of the dripping water was erratic and each time a drop hit, it echoed like a fire cracker exploding in a concrete canyon.

Beneath her boots, the ground was strewn with huge rocks made extremely slippery by a thick coat of moisture. As Maura carefully made her way forward, she kept her left hand on the wall of the mineshaft to hold herself steady, while her right gripped the flashlight.

As much as she wanted to find Quint, she didn't want to

take the risk of falling. If the baby was harmed, Quint would never forgive her. Nor would she ever forgive herself.

After traveling about ten yards deeper into the cavern, the air grew stuffier and the path ahead abruptly split in two directions. Since one still held the tracks to carry ore cars, Maura followed it and prayed she'd chosen the right one.

With a few more yards behind her, she paused, peered into the eerie darkness and willed him to answer. "Quint? Are you in here? It's Maura!"

Suddenly from far away, the muffled sound of his voice came back to her.

"Maura! Stay there! I'm coming!"

The relief pouring through her was so great she was practically sobbing by the time he finally reached her side.

"Oh, Quint!" she exclaimed. "Are you all right? What are you doing in here? You told me this mine wasn't safe to enter!"

Grabbing her by the shoulders, he tugged her to him. "It isn't! So why are you in here?"

"Because I came out here to find you. When I couldn't, I decided you must have come in here. I was afraid, Quint! If you'd been lying hurt or trapped—" Shuddering, she broke off as tears of relief poured down her face.

With a choked groan, he clutched her tight against him and buried his face in her hair. The intensity of his grip dazed her, made her wonder what he could possibly be thinking.

"Maura, Maura," he whispered. "I'm sorry I frightened you. But you shouldn't have come in here. If something happened to you or the baby—well, I don't even want to think about it!"

Lifting her head from his chest, she searched his face in the semidarkness. "Do you mean that, Quint?"

"Why wouldn't I mean it? You're my wife. You're carrying my child—a child I can't wait to hold in my arms."

Fresh tears spiked her lashes and poured from the corners of her eyes. "I was afraid you wanted a divorce," she finally managed to get out.

Stunned, he shook his head, then grabbed her by the arm. "Let's get out of this dark hole. We'll talk about this outside."

"No! I'm fine right here," she said stubbornly. "And I'm not going anywhere! Not until we discuss this!"

Releasing a long breath, he asked, "Why would you think I wanted a divorce?"

"Since we returned from our honeymoon you haven't seemed too happy to be around me. I've been thinking that you must be regretting that we married. And then—" Biting down on her lip, she glanced away from him and into the darkness. "Earlier this evening, before I left work, Bridget confessed to me that she'd seen you coming out of a lawyer's office. I thought—"

"The worst," he finished grimly, then groaned deep in his throat. "Oh, Maura, can't you see I'd wither away without you?"

Confusion clouded her eyes. "No, Quint. I've been seeing a very unhappy man trying to pretend that everything is okay."

"I guess that's true. But only because after we got home from Hawaii I realized just how very much I loved you. And I knew you didn't feel the same. That you'd only married me because of the baby." His fingers tightened against her back until she was pressed so close to him that she could feel his heart beating against hers, his warm breath brushing her cheek. "Have I ruined every chance for us? Tell me I haven't!"

She said in a strained voice, "Oh, Quint—you haven't ruined anything. I'm the one who's been an idiot."

"Not as much as I've been," he mouthed against her cheek. "I should have told you that I went to see the lawyer to make sure my will was in order. If anything should happen to me there won't be any doubt about my wishes. My whole estate will go to you and our child."

Overwhelmed, she clutched his shoulders and choked back a sob. "We hadn't been together too long when the baby happened. And I knew you weren't looking for a family back then. I felt very guilty about getting pregnant and—"

"Oh, God, Maura, do you know how happy I am that you did get pregnant? That wasn't an accident by any fault of yours, that was dealt by a higher hand. He meant for the baby to cement us together."

Everything inside of her was shaking, trembling with a joy so great she wanted to shout. "Quint, I love you. So very much. As long as you want me as your wife, I—"

"Want you? Oh, darling, I love you! Love you with all my heart." His head bent and his lips suddenly hovered over hers. "I should have told you that from the very beginning. Instead, I kept denying the way I was feeling. I didn't want to be that needy or vulnerable. I told myself it was your body that I was infatuated with and that if or when you decided to get up and walk away from me, I could stand it, I wouldn't be hurt. But when we got back from our honeymoon the reality of being home—of being married—shook my eyes wide-open, made me see that nothing would matter if I didn't have you in my world."

Amazed that he was saying these things to her, she

reached up and framed his face with her hands. "But you've acted so distant and—"

"Because I was scared. I could see you were unhappy and that I'd forced you into a marriage you hadn't wanted. So I dove into my work and tried to pretend I didn't care. God, I've been stupid!"

Her thumbs caressed the lines of fatigue beneath his eyes. "You were right. I've been unhappy, too. I didn't want to get married. Because I wanted you to marry me for love—not just because of the baby. But you never mentioned the word to me."

"Neither did you," he countered. "You said you'd slept with me for the sex. You can't possibly know how much that cut me, Maura."

"I'm sorry, Quint, truly. But after Gil crushed me, I couldn't believe a man like you could actually love me. And I was trying to hang on to what little pride I had left."

His mouth twisted ruefully. "And I was thinking that after three years of being with Holly, of believing she loved me, I lost her. How the hell did I think I could possibly hang on to you? Especially when you didn't want to marry me in the first place."

Suddenly, happy laughter bubbled up inside her and once it passed her lips, the sound rippled through the old gold mine like musical notes. "Holly, Gil. We can forgive and forget the mistakes we made with them, darling. None of that matters anymore. Because you and I have so much more than they could have ever given us. We have each other."

With a growl of contentment, his hand dropped to her belly and as he pressed his hand lovingly against their child, he whispered, "And we have our baby."

"Our baby," she repeated.

Closing the last bit of space between their lips, Quint let his kiss tell Maura how much he loved and wanted her and would until he died.

"Now," he said when he finally lifted his head, "don't you think it's time we got out of this place? It's probably full of rattlesnakes and bats and everything else."

With a sly little smile, she squeezed his hand. "As soon as you tell me why you were in here, we'll leave. Jake said you received a phone call and then you took off for the mine. Did Abe send you out here?"

He chuckled. "I like to please my grandfather, but not that much. We had a huge row about the mine last night. He's adamant that we need to start mining it again. I tried to explain all the reasons I didn't want to do that and told him flat out that my mind was made up. I was going to board this place up and forget it completely."

"Looks like you sure told him how the cow eats the corn," Maura said wryly.

"Well, this afternoon I had a change of heart. My brother Mac called. And he sagely pointed out that I needed to quit fighting my love for you."

"Mmm. Next time I see your brother, I'm going to tell him what a wise, wise man he is."

Smiling, Quint smoothed her hair back and placed a kiss on her soft forehead. "He also implied that I should quit fighting Grandfather's dreams. After all, Abe got what he has by taking risks."

"So you've decided to reopen this thing and let the miners start digging again?"

He nodded. "After I talked with Mac, I felt compelled to come out here. And once I got here, it was like a voice was calling me inside. That's when I decided I'd come in here and see for myself if any sort of structure to the shaft was left. I was surprised to see it's in better condition than I expected. 'Course it will take lots of shoring before actual mining can begin, but Gramps is willing to make the investment and so am I."

"I'm glad, Quint. I think someday you'll see what a gift you're giving your grandfather by going along with this. And we owe him so much, darling, for bringing us together. Don't you think?"

Quint opened his mouth to answer just as an odd rumble sounded a few feet above their heads.

Frowning, Maura asked, "Was that thunder? I didn't notice any clouds when I drove up."

Quint tilted his head to one side as the both of them listened intently. "I don't know what it was," he said, "Maybe—"

He broke off as a grumbling ache suddenly belched through the mine shaft. The sound of cracking wood splintered the air and choking dust showered down from the ceiling.

"Hurry! We'd better get out of here. Hold on to me!"

Grabbing her hand, he rushed her in the direction of the entrance. But they'd hardly taken ten strides when the ground and the walls begin to shake with an intensity that caused Maura to scream and fling herself against Quint.

"Oh, God! It's an earthquake! It's going to collapse on us!"

She'd hardly gotten the words out when a portion of the ceiling above their heads started to fall. Taking Maura with him, Quint leaped to one side of the cavern, then after pushing her to a crouch, he covered her body as best as he could with his own.

Two feet away, a heavy beam broke, to send the jagged

ends stabbing into the floor of the cave. Rocks, dirt and gravel spilled from the gaping hole like a landslide roaring down a mountain. The sound was deafening.

Dust boiled around them so thick they both began to cough and sputter for air. Maura buried her face deeper in the middle of Quint's chest, while she felt the protection of his arms circle tightly around her. And in that moment she knew that no matter what happened in their lives, Quint loved her, would always love her.

After what seemed like an eternity, all went quiet. The dust and rock settled. And Quint slowly raised the both of them to their feet.

Totally dazed, Maura clung to Quint's arm as she glanced around at the rubble piled in the middle of the mine shaft. "Whew! That was close!"

Quint pointed his flashlight toward the heap of ore that had fallen from the cave-in. Some of the rocks and debris had rolled all the way to their feet. But by the grace of God, neither of them appeared to be hurt.

"Close, I'll say," Quint agreed.

While he took off his hat and wiped his grimy forehead on the back of his sleeve, Maura attempted to shake the dirt and pebbles from her hair. She was swiping the grime away from her eyes, when some sort of flash caught her attention and she took a second look at the rocks strewn about their feet.

"Quint, shine your light down here. Something looks—" Frowning, she bent down and picked up one of the larger pieces of ore. "It's sparkling like—"

Excitement flickered, then rushed over her as she yelped out an incredible laugh. "It's gold, Quint! This old mine wasn't trying to kill us. It was trying to tell us it was never empty of riches." She grabbed his arm. "Let's go show Abe what we've found!"

Too stunned to speak, Quint stuffed two of the rocks into his pocket, then reached for Maura's hand.

Finally, he managed to say, "Looks like we've struck it rich, honey. But as far as I'm concerned my treasure is you."

Happy tears stung Maura's eyes as her husband led her out of the darkness of the mine and into the brightness of their love.

## *Epilogue*

A year to the day later, on a bright fall afternoon, Maura and Quint stood on the sidewalk of the old Chillicothe general store, while just behind them, Abe had his seven-month-old great-grandson, Riley Donovan Cantrell, cradled in one arm.

The group of four had just enjoyed a picnic lunch at the same table where Maura and Quint had eaten that day the storm had struck and little Riley had been conceived. Now that the meal was over, Abe insisted they all walk over to the mine site and let the baby watch the large equipment at work.

Once Red Bluff Mining Company had moved in, the crew had quickly gone to work to make the mine a safe workplace. Even going at a rapid pace that enormous task had taken a few months. After the shoring had been completed, the miners had finally gone in to dig and much to everyone's dismay had discovered a rich vein of gold that was expected to reach far back into the mountainside. Geologists predicted it would take years to recover all of the yellow metal inside the Golden Spur.

Maura's older brother Conall, a rancher and business-man in his own right, had agreed to take over the management of the mine operations, which thankfully left Quint free to do the things he loved to do, which was work with his cattle and horses.

Up until Riley had been born, Maura had continued to work at Bridget's clinic, but now she was content to stay at home and be a mother…a job that more than agreed with her. She'd never been happier or felt more fulfilled, and each time she looked at her husband, it showed on her face. Maybe someday, after their family was grown, she would return to being a nurse. But for now, she simply wanted to be a wife and mother.

As the four of them left the old ghost town and walked toward the low mountain ridge where the mine entrance was located, Quint asked his grandfather, "Would you like for me to carry Riley? He can get heavy."

"Nope. My little cowboy is not that heavy. Yet."

"He will be if you keep stuffing his face with those animal cookies," Quint said drily.

Smiling, Maura glanced at Abe and her young son. Soggy cookie crumbs smeared the baby's plump cheeks and the front of Abe's shirt, but the old man hardly cared about keeping either of them tidy. He adored his great-grandson and had taken to visiting the Golden Spur on a regular basis in order to spend more time with him.

For safety purposes, the entrance to the mine and the excavated area around it was now enclosed with a tall, chain-link fence. As for any cattle that roamed near the mine, Quint had fenced off the outer portion of the working area and the road to the highway in order to keep the animals from grazing too close to the truck traffic.

In a way, the mine had caused more work to be done to the ranch, but the benefits of the gold sales far superseded the cost and trouble. So far the income from the gold had been extraordinary and Quint and Maura were now sharing part of the earnings with both their families and putting the remainder away for Riley and the other children they hoped to have soon. As for Abe, he didn't want any money. It was enough for him to see his dreams come true.

Now as they stood outside the fence and watched the men and equipment at work, Abe said, "I knew all along there was a vein of gold left in these hills. Back in the fifties, when they quit this mine, they shouldn't have stopped lookin'. A man can't stop searchin'. Not when he truly believes in somethin'."

Gazing down at Maura, Quint curled his arm lovingly around the back of her waist. "I'll agree with that."

Seeing the look his grandson was giving his wife, Abe snorted. "Don't go actin' like you findin' Maura and a mine full of gold was all your idea. If I'd left things up to you, you'd still be single and the old Spur would be boarded up and forgotten."

Grinning faintly, Quint shook his head. "Oh. So you think you're responsible for getting me a wife?"

"Damned right," Abe retorted. "Why do you think I hired Maura in the first place?"

Quint winked at Maura. "Because you had dizzy spells."

Abe let out another snort. "Hell, no! I knew how to treat myself for those spells. I wanted her for you." Suddenly his eyes misted over and after clearing his throat, he bent his head and placed a kiss on the top of Riley's sandy red curls. "You see," he said in a voice thick with emotion, "I had big dreams for you, Quint. And I've been blessed to see them all come true."

Except for the first time he'd held Riley in his arms, Maura had never seen Abe get teary-eyed over anything. Seeing his softer side, she couldn't help but get a little blurry-eyed herself. As she watched Abe move away from them and carry little Riley over to the flimsy shade of a pinyon tree, she smiled through her tears. Her son. Her husband. Her family. She had everything she'd ever wanted.

The tug of Quint's hand at the side of her waist brought Maura's head back around to her husband and she glanced slyly up at him. "Has your grandfather always been such a conniver?"

"Yes. But I like to think that somehow, someway, I would have found you in spite of his help." He bent his head and softly kissed her lips. "You know, that first time we went riding together and you made such a big deal out of the cholla blooms was the first time I'd ever looked at the ranch through different eyes. You made me see that I needed to stop and appreciate the beauty around me. And then later, after we married, you made me realize that the Golden Spur wasn't just a place for me to work, to raise herds of cattle and horses. It was a place for us to live and love and raise our children. You taught me how to dream, my darling. And you've made mine all come true. Don't ever forget that."

Sometimes when her husband touched her, she felt so full of love that she was overwhelmed with the urge to show him, tell him exactly how much he meant to her. And then, like this very moment, she knew her feelings were so deep it was impossible to express them. So she simply smiled and pressed her cheek against his chest.

"You know," she said softly, "I think this is the perfect time to tell Abe he's going to be great-grandfather again. Don't you?"

"I think it's the perfect time," Quint agreed.

Hand in hand, they walked over to give Abe the good news.

\* \* \* \* \*

*Stella Bagwell and Silhouette Special Edition
invite you to come back to Lincoln County in April
to discover what happens when Brady
rescues a young woman who's lost her memory!*

*Fan favorite Leslie Kelly is bringing her readers a fantasy so scandalous, we're calling it FORBIDDEN!*

*Look for
PLAY WITH ME
Available February 2010 from Harlequin® Blaze™.*

"AREN'T YOU GOING TO SAY 'Fly me' or at least 'Welcome Aboard'?"

Amanda Bauer didn't. The softly muttered word that actually came out of her mouth was a lot less welcoming. And had fewer letters. Four, to be exact.

The man shook his head and tsked. "Not exactly the friendly skies. Haven't caught the spirit yet this morning?"

"Make one more airline-slogan crack and you'll be walking to Chicago," she said.

He nodded once, then pushed his sunglasses onto the top of his tousled hair. The move revealed blue eyes that matched the sky above. And yeah. They were twinkling. Damn it.

"Understood. Just, uh, promise me you'll say 'Coffee, tea or me' at least once, okay? Please?"

Amanda tried to glare, but that twinkle sucked the annoyance right out of her. She could only draw in a slow breath as he climbed into the plane. As she watched her passenger disappear into the small jet, she had to wonder about the trip she was about to take.

Coffee and tea they had, and he was welcome to them. But her? Well, she'd never even considered making a move on a customer before. Talk about unprofessional.

And yet…

Something inside her suddenly wanted to take a chance, to be a little outrageous.

How long since she had done indecent things—or decent ones, for that matter—with a sexy man? Not since before they'd thrown all their energies into expanding Clear-Blue Air, at the very least. She hadn't had time for a lunch date, much less the kind of lust-fest she'd enjoyed in her younger years. The kind that lasted for entire weekends and involved not leaving a bed except to grab the kind of sensuous food that could be smeared onto—and eaten off—someone else's hot, naked, sweat-tinged body.

She closed her eyes, her hand clenching tight on the railing. Her heart fluttered in her chest and she tried to make herself move. But she couldn't—not climbing up, but not backing away, either. Not physically, and not in her head.

Was she really considering this? God, she hadn't even looked at the stranger's left hand to make sure he was available. She had no idea if he was actually attracted to her or just an irrepressible flirt. Yet something inside was telling her to take a shot with this man.

It was crazy. Something she'd never considered. Yet right now, at this moment, she was definitely considering it. If he was available…could she do it? Seduce a stranger. Have an anonymous fling, like something out of a blue movie on late-night cable?

She didn't know. All she knew was that the flight to Chicago was a short one so she had to decide quickly. And as she put her foot on the bottom step and began to climb up, Amanda suddenly had to wonder if she was about to embark on the ride of her life.

Sold, bought, bargained for or bartered

*He'll take his…*

## *Bride on Approval*

Whether there's a debt to be paid,
a will to be obeyed or a business
to be saved…she has no choice
but to say, "I do"!

# PURE PRINCESS, BARTERED BRIDE
### by *Caitlin Crews*
#### #2894

*Available February 2010!*

**ESCAPE AROUND the WORLD**

*Dream destinations, whirlwind weddings!*

*The Daredevil Tycoon*

*by*

# BARBARA McMAHON

A hot-air balloon race with Amalia Catalon's sexy daredevil boss, Rafael Sandoval, is only the beginning of her exciting Spanish adventure....

*Available in January 2010
wherever books are sold.*

Welcome to Montana—the home of bold men and daring women, where tales of passion, adventure and intrigue unfold beneath the Big Sky.

## *Rogue Stallion* by DIANA PALMER

Undaunted by rogue cop Sterling McCallum's heart of stone and his warnings to back off, Jessica Larson stands her ground, braving the rising emotions between them until the mystery of his past comes to the surface.

*Montana* ★ MAVERICKS™
### RETURN TO BIG SKY COUNTRY

*Available in January 2010 wherever you buy books.*

# HARLEQUIN
## *Ambassadors*

## *Want to share your passion for reading Harlequin® Books?*

### Become a Harlequin Ambassador!

Harlequin Ambassadors are a group of passionate and well-connected readers who are willing to share their joy of reading Harlequin® books with family and friends.

You'll be sent all the tools you need to spark great conversation, including free books!

All we ask is that you share the romance with your friends and family!

You'll also be invited to have a say in new book ideas and exchange opinions with women just like you!

### To see if you qualify* to be a Harlequin Ambassador, please visit
### www.HarlequinAmbassadors.com.

*Please note that not everyone who applies to be a Harlequin Ambassador will qualify. For more information please visit www.HarlequinAmbassadors.com.

### Thank you for your participation.

BAP09BPA